UNDER
HER THUMB

UNDER HER THUMB
EROTIC STORIES OF
FEMALE DOMINATION

EDITED BY
D. L. KING

FOREWORD BY
MIDORI

Published in the United States by Cleis Press, Inc., 2246 Sixth Street, Berkeley, California 94710.

Printed in the United States.
Cover design: Scott Idleman/Blink
Cover photograph: Chris Gramly/Getty Images
Text design: Frank Wiedemann

First Edition.
10 9 8 7 6 5 4 3 2 1

Trade paper ISBN: 978-1-57344-927-4
E-book ISBN: 978-1-57344-944-1

Contents

FOREWORD

Midori

She is a towering idol and a derided caricature.

Her presence is desired and denied.

She is glorified and complicated beyond her reality and debased and reduced in spite of her truth.

Her true form, however, stands quietly in the stillness, in the eye of the storm; a storm of opinion, fear, lust, anger, misogyny, feminism, sexism, power, media, myth, fantasy, religion, arousal, guilt, passion, mistrust, awe, anxiety and yearning.

She is the dominant woman.

Often she's recognized only for, and reduced to, the superficial signifiers of costume and accessories: high heels, leather, corsets and whips of the "Dominatrix" fashion genre. While garments and accessories have their own potential for potent power and pleasure[1], they are not what make the dominant woman. Sadly *She* has been substituted so often with these clichés that those

---

1   Valerie Steele, *Fetish: Fashion, Sex and Power* (Oxford University Press, 1997).

craving to possess, or be possessed by *Her power* jump to the misguided conclusion that simply donning these garments will automatically bring forth power. Then they wonder, crestfallen at the underwhelming outcome, "Is that all there is?" Perhaps we've given too much totemic power to the objects at the cost of seeing the true source of *Her* power.[2]

The energy source of the dominant femme is not the artifice of costumes. The truth of *Her* is the brutal honesty of, and to, her desires, deliberately shaped by equally fierce self-discipline. She must intentionally engage this self-discipline, as it's necessary to resist capitulation to lifelong social conditioning and cultural pressures of constant self-effacing and denial of yearnings.

It may seem contradictory that self-discipline would be necessary for the dominant woman to be satisfied. Doesn't she just have to demand what she wants? First, this assumes that making a demand equates to authority. Any tantrum-throwing three-year-old can demand what she wants, but that's not going to get results. The brat child has no authority. Pestering others until they give in is merely juvenile manipulation. Authority, however, comes with knowledge, a grasp of resources and limits, respect, and understanding of one's scope of influence. Second, the statement assumes that the woman truly knows what she wants. So often we, men and women alike, accept what we are told we should want, never examining our true desires. Women, in particular, are often trained from childhood that stating our own wants is undesirable and wicked. Women are rewarded for sublimating primary wants into providing for others. Want to be adored? You're adored only after you adore another. Want to enjoy power? You access power by enabling others to be

---

2   Midori, *Wild Side Sex: The Book of Kink* (Daedalus Publishing, 2005).

powerful. Want an orgasm? You better know how to create a great orgasm in another. Her pleasures are then reduced to the currency of erotic bartering, or maybe just an afterthought, like a tip, for which she should be grateful. Her true hungers, if voiced or demanded, are scolded as selfish and cruel. A woman stating her want makes others intensely uncomfortable. We are taught to live a lie for the sake of others' comfort. Being honest can be profoundly difficult for many women.

There has to be another way, a way of honesty.

So *She* must deeply and fully examine what she really wants. This, of course, isn't easy when there are so many years and layers of social conditioning to dig through.

So often I hear, from women who perform the actions of dominance, whip in hand and cruel words falling from their lips, that despite these actions, they feel lost and unfulfilled— they haven't figured out what they really want, much less how to demand it. When the lover says, "But she's a dominant woman, she should know what she wants," he's blithely blind to the hard work it takes for her to truly open her eyes and heart. Self-discipline is vital to the femme dom; she must abstain from merely aping dominance to please a partner or feed into his or her expectations. It is important to examine her deepest desires if she wants to make them a reality. Are wanton cruelty, anger and malice necessary in the dominant woman? No. Once *Her* desires are explored and expressed, how they are actualized will vary as wildly as the women themselves. Her dominance may range from sweet and quiet to severe and punishing. They are all valid as long as she is true to her self.

The femme dom as filled with rage and hate, engaging in vulgarity and thoughtless violence, is a stereotype used to dismiss the complexity of women's desires. It's high time we leave that behind.

Another truth, and challenge, of the dominant femme is finding a partner who willingly and joyously enters into a relationship with her. In the erotic dance of dominance and submission, there must be a worthy partner of quality and self-discipline equal to hers. An individual merely stating that he or she is a submissive isn't going to attract a great dominant. A partner who inflames the passions and incites the deep dominant hungers in *Her* isn't just *anybody*—he or she has to be *somebody*. True surrender and belonging comes from a place of self-knowledge, agency, choice and powerful devotion.

The dominant woman: *She* is her own truth and her finest creation. To love and woo her is to enter into a realm, brilliantly real and tantalizingly raw, full of unexpected and vivid pleasures.

INTRODUCTION

I recently bought myself an expensive new toy: something I've been lusting after for several years, but never felt I could afford. When I found myself with a bit of extra cash, and saw the ET 312B offered at a really good price, I bit the bullet and decided to just go for it.

I hadn't managed to put it away by the time my former computer boy came over to help with a project. We haven't had a dominant/submissive relationship in several years, but when we did, he worked in exchange for the privilege of being spanked.

When we'd gotten as much work done as we could, we called it an evening and retired to the living room to chat and catch up on life (I hadn't seen him in a long time). I noticed the unit sitting under the coffee table. Still very excited about my new purchase, I pointed to it and said, "Look what I got." He knew I'd always wanted one.

He smiled and blushed a little, fidgeted and mentioned that he'd already noticed it; in fact, it was the first thing to draw his attention when he sat down on the couch. He got a wistful look and licked his lips. I think we were both thinking, *Yeah, well, that would have been fun...* You see: we don't have that kind of relationship anymore.

So, why am I mentioning it?

The bond of bottom and top; boy and ma'am; sub and domme, never really goes away. There's something very profound—even spiritual—about a dominant/submissive relationship that sticks with you, whether it's a fully committed, loving relationship or a casual, purely platonic one. Even if the sexual aspect ends, the bond remains.

I think it may be even more so in the case of male submissives and female dominants. I think people who identify as male, regardless of gender, tend to feel things more deeply than what we are conditioned to believe is stereotypical. Men have been thrust into situations of strength and made to play the part, whether it's natural or not. When those societal restraints are released, a man can let out his buried feelings of submission and allow himself (or be forced to allow himself, if that makes it easier) to experience the things he craves in the darkest recesses of his mind. It's that depth that I've found in these stories. Whether they're about intense, mutually respectful relationships, like the one in Andrea Zanin's "Quiet," or more casual, although highly ritualistic forms of entertainment, like the scenes in Laura Antoniou's "Blame *Spartacus*," it's clear there's something important going on.

A man's worshipful description of the relationship he has with his dominant becomes all the more intimate when we find they have been married for many years in Lawrence Westerman's "Her Majesty's Plaything." Though it can be just as compelling, sometimes even more so, when it isn't coming from a lifetime commitment, but from a simple need to serve,

to be humbled, to be humiliated and dominated, like in Lisabet
Sarai's "Layover." And then there are the pros. Poor Nate is
going crazy. He can't get his mistress out of his head.

> *Kendall was the mistress of his dreams. He knew he*
> *was lucky to have her. She was remote, ice blonde*
> *and elegant: Grace Kelly with a whip. She never*
> *had sex with him, because she had no interest in his*
> *cock. He'd been her sub for seven months and he'd*
> *still never seen her naked. He dreamed of that and*
> *dreamed of fucking her too. He rationalized that his*
> *enforced chastity was for the best, that sex with her*
> *would take him from obsession to full madness. He*
> *would want her all the time then, he would weep*
> *and howl and beg for more until she cut him off.*
>
> *But one night she cut him off anyhow, and all his*
> *worst predictions came true.*

Kendall's cutting Nate off made him unable to function. He
needs to exorcise her from his head. His best friend suggests
a pro but Nate doesn't think of them as true mistresses. The
simple act of "paying for it," according to Nate, makes him the
top—not at all what he wants to be. He's in for an education
when he meets Valerie Alexander's "La Sexorcista."

And, by the way, not all the submissives in this book are
male. Women dominating women can make me just as weak in
the knees as women dominating men. I'm pretty sure you'll feel
the same when you read Evan Mora's "Uncharted Territory" or
Anne Grip's "The Dinner Party."

When I put an anthology together, I only include stories that
grab me, or make me want to put them down and do something
other than read. The stories in *Under Her Thumb* are special.

These are stories I can relate to in a personal way. They make me yearn; they make me laugh; they make me dream. They combine with my own psyche, my experience and my fantasies.

If the thought of a powerful woman makes you weak with want, or the idea of a boy kept under tight control reminds you of the very power you crave, then I hope you will find this book as personally appealing as I do.

D. L. King
New York City

QUIET

Andrea Zanin

It is dark. Quiet. She can hear his breathing, close, as she keeps one hand on his chest so that his naked back, bruised from the beating she gave him a mere half hour earlier at the club, is pressed against the coolness of the bedroom wall. She bats his tentative hand away, not wanting to be touched tonight.

Tonight, she has been on display. This was not her intention. It doesn't matter that she dressed up for her own pleasure; it doesn't matter that she dressed him for her pleasure as well. The deliciousness of her curves encased in a boned corset made her feel austere, strict. The formfitting leather pencil skirt was elegant. His presence at her side, at her feet, was the correct order of things. But the public clubs are full of people who do not know what they are looking at. They are populated by men who see only their fantasies come to life, not the flesh-and-blood women in front of them. These men do not notice his devotion, or his beauty. They see only her, and only her contours, at that. A convenient body upon which to build a scenario of shrill domination, one that just happens to cater to the whims of those who think they wish to obey. She has spent too much time as a projection screen with an hourglass figure. She is angry. And she is also aroused. He has been attentive all evening. His softness makes her harder, sharper. His obedience touches some wire inside her, one that runs from her mind directly to her sex, and sets it humming as though electrified. His acquiescence never fails to awaken her hunger. His simple wordless presence reminds her that men are not all blind. Tonight, he took the pain she bestowed upon him, the sweetest of gifts, knowing that it had an edge that was not about him at all. He absorbed her slow, simmering rage and turned it into a tool of pleasure, his and hers—the transformative magic of the masochist. This, he offered willingly, and she accepted, funneling her frustration into the skilled wielding of her favorite implements, painting the colors of her desire on his flesh, soft and strong.

Now, she gestures at him not to move. Unhooks the restrictive corset, peels off the sweat-sticky leather skirt. Free of her self-imposed bondage, she is not exposed, but all the more powerful. Her knee-high boots, gleaming dully in the faint white of the streetlamp outside, keep her almost as tall as his six feet.

She slowly strokes the shaved slickness of his chest, the motion almost creates a purr. She plays her fingertips and soft scratches of her nails against his sensitive nipples, hears his breath go deeper as she draws them toward her, twists her knuckles around them, pulls and kneads until she's stretching his skin into painful points of burning, hurting pleasure. Even in the dark, she can see his achingly erect cock making a distorted shape underneath the knee-length black skirt he donned for the evening.

She slides her fingernails up the back of his warm neck to grip his scalp—his heavy, soft, long hair like velvet against her forearm—and guides him to the bed, motions for him to slip off the skirt and lie down. He hangs it tidily from the footboard before stretching out like a cat exposing its belly.

She lifts her leg and places one spike heel on the mattress, dangerously close to his swollen crotch, the tip of her toe just brushing his hairless inner thigh, and relishes the sight of his vulnerability straining against the black fishnets.

He's a quiet one. A trace of lipstick remains on his parted lips as he inhales, exhales, acknowledging that he's now the one who is on display. This audience is the only one that matters. Her gaze is the one through which he wants to be seen. His chest leaps shallowly in the faint shadows. She watches, calculating. He watches her watch him, questions in his mouth not released.

Were it not for her tiny thong, her wetness would be leaving clear, glistening trails on her thighs. Impatient with her own body, she abruptly moves her foot away. She reaches down brusquely, inserts a fingernail into a hole in his nylons and neatly rips one leg from crotch to toe in a swift motion. She sends his back into an arch when she leans over and sinks her teeth into the flesh of his big toe—he almost whimpers, but catches himself. His cock throbs visibly. She lacerates the other leg of the fishnets, the sound tearing the night. She rewards him for his delightful shiver by sliding her hand up between his legs for a firm squeeze. In turn he rises to her touch, his hardness so full she can feel every contour of the head, the warm shaft, the small pouchy frenulum, even through the lace of his panties.

This is not humiliation. There is nothing humiliating about being beautiful or about being feminine. She, herself, is both of those things, and many more. She cannot fathom how encouraging these qualities in others could possibly be shameful or worthy of mockery. There is also nothing humiliating about submission. It is a gift and all the finer when given selectively. She relishes these aspects of him, both of them, separate and entwined, and has taught him to be proud of them. When he at first thought he needed to play a silly role, to be a sissy or to giggle like a schoolgirl, she corrected him firmly. There would be no need for such undignified behavior. He would be graceful and humble in his pride. He would see himself through her eyes as a refined creature, a valuable specimen, a work of art. A treasured piece of property to be polished, cared for and thoroughly used to the best of her capacity.

The men at the clubs do not see him. Sometimes they don't notice him at all, too focused on her to bother registering the presence of a partner. Sometimes, when they do notice him, they assume that his demurely feminine attire is a punishment, or a fetish, or an attempt on her part to make him into something less than he is. This offends her. It is quite the contrary. She is simply enhancing what he already is and very much wants to be. She knows he is beautiful. He knows she is right.

She motions for him to sit upright, arranges the pillows against the headboard and slides onto the bed behind him, one leg on each side of his body. She pulls him back so his narrow hips settle close to her and his tender back rests against her breasts. Quite deliberately, she raises her feet, one at a time, and presses each boot heel into the delicate, now-bare white flesh of his lean thighs.

She winds up a fistful of his luscious hair and raises his ear to her mouth. She speaks two words in low tones, and he hesitates a moment before reaching his long fingers into the panties. He draws them down to expose his near-purple length and begins to stroke himself. The too-small lace still cups his testicles, and she growls low in her throat at the sight.

He writhes as her fingertips catch again at his sore nipples, but his stroking speeds up as she works her fingernails into the silky areolae and draws up to flick the tiny hard points over and over. His body tenses and his hand moves more quickly still as his back becomes rigid, pressing his welted skin into her softness. He is marked, claimed, the blossoming red and purple flowers under his skin an elegant reminder of her ownership of that flesh.

She wonders if perhaps she should stop attending the club events. They are painful. He might be sad, as there are few places he can go wearing the clothes that are most becoming to him, showing his face at its most lovely. But his loveliness is wasted on those who do not know what they are seeing. He deserves better. She deserves better as well. And yet, the spaces in which they can be themselves are rare, and precious, even if flawed. To what extent should one settle for less than what one wants, when what one wants may not exist? To what extent should one allow one's property to be exposed to the harsh elements, when that exposure also offers the rare opportunity for nourishment? She is not accustomed to settling.

A knot inside her twists tighter as she bares her teeth and bites deeply into the sinewy place where his neck curves into his shoulder, and a tiny strangled pleading sound finally escapes his throat. She breathes her permission, and he shoots uncontrollably in silver streaks up his smooth belly to his sternum, an offering for her to enjoy.

She is full, her body wanting to be emptied, her mind resolutely resisting. She pushes away the urge. Disengages her boot heels from where they have made deep depressions in his thighs, hooks her foot behind his knee and flips him efficiently onto his side. He cannot see her face. She nudges him into a fetal position and curls up behind him, his sweet ass against her heat, which she refuses to press into him. With her cheekbone against the flat place between his shoulder blades, she lies awake, stroking his hip and allowing him to drift. It's dark, quiet. She does not sleep.

LA SEXORCISTA

Valerie Alexander

N ate liked suffering. He liked it a lot. He liked the sting of a crop on his thighs and the abrasion of carpet on his nipples, followed by the cut of Kendall's insults. He liked the initial strike of a cane on his bottom and the secondary bloom of pain through his body. He loved being slapped across the face and called a filthy slut boy right before he came, against Kendall's orders, thereby earning more blows from her hairbrush.

"I really love you," he would mutter into the leather of her boots, right before the steel-reinforced toe kicked him off.

Kendall was the mistress of his dreams. He knew he was lucky to have her. She was remote, ice blonde and elegant: Grace Kelly with a whip. She never had sex with him, because she had no interest in his cock. He'd been her sub for seven months and he'd still never seen her naked. He dreamed of that and dreamed of fucking her too. He rationalized that his enforced chastity was for the best, that sex with her would take him from obsession to full madness. He would want her all the time then, he would weep and howl and beg for more until she cut him off.

But one night she cut him off anyhow, and all his worst predictions came true.

"I need help," is what he said on the phone to his friend Patrick. "I will do anything to drive her out of my mind."

"She won't talk to you?"

"Oh, she'll talk. We've talked about it. She just says she's bored and needs something new."

"See a pro domme, Nate. Just shell out the cash and do it."

"Pro dommes don't work for me. The fact that I'm paying, the whole checklist the dungeon does—I might as well be giving instructions to my housecleaner. I can never forget that I'm the one in control."

There the matter lay for another nine days of agony, nine days of pining for Kendall's silver-backed hairbrush and the exhilarating thrill of her scorn, until he could barely distinguish the rawness of his fingers from the chafing of his cock. Then Patrick came through for him with a phone number.

"They call her La Sexorcista, because she can make you forget anyone. She's good—she knows how to get inside your head."

"A pro is a pro, even with a fancy hook. And a ridiculous one, I have to say."

"Just schedule a session, Nate. It's not like you can't afford it."

In the end he did it, only to prove how futile it would be. He didn't speak to the dominatrix herself; an assistant, probably one of her real subs, made the appointment. And an odd one it was, the address an abandoned gas station in a bad part of town. "So she's going to pick me up or what...?"

"Just go into the gas station. She'll direct you from there."

Paranoid scenarios ran through his mind, but the very act of agreeing to the abandoned gas station had sparked his interest. If throwing him off balance was part of her game, La Sexorcista—or Sofia as her real name was—was off to a clever start. That Friday night he arrived at the gas station. It was dark and locked, the disconnected pumps ghostly in the night. He waited outside in the humid dark until a police cruiser slowed down enough to eye him suspiciously. He circled the back of the station, where he found an unlocked door.

He entered a dark room redolent of gasoline and tires. Enough streetlight spilled through the windows to illuminate the cement floor, a pair of coveralls on a hook, shelves and a long table. It was definitely not a converted dungeon. That was clear from the oil stains and the faint ghost of automotive fluids lingering in the air. Kendall wouldn't have been caught dead here.

Boot steps clicked on the cement floor. He turned to see the pro domme walking out of the shadows. So this was La Sexorcista. She was Mexican and she was pretty and above her black thigh-high boots, she was naked. That was all he could see at first, full breasts and a soft stomach curving into round hips, and bare skin everywhere he looked. She had almond-shaped eyes that were black as obsidian and loose dark hair that waved past her nipples.

She didn't carry a riding crop or a single tail or even cuffs. A sinking feeling went through him. She was just a hooker, a hooker with a hook, who thought a first-class professional fuck would be enough to exorcise Kendall's memory. It wouldn't. She didn't understand submissive men at all.

"Don't talk," she said. Her voice was coolly indifferent, not scornful like Kendall's. "I am Sofia. You speak only when I ask you to, and you call me Mistress. Understand?"

"Yes, Mistress."

"Go into the corner where that chair is and get undressed. Fold your clothes neatly in a pile. Then come back here on your knees."

Apparently they weren't going to go over the safeword he'd given her assistant, or any kind of rules. Well, then. This was nothing like the dungeons he'd tried when he was younger, but so far it was titillating.

He resisted the urge to look back at her as he undressed. A naked pro domme. That was a first. It wasn't that he didn't like vanilla sex—he did, and he liked cuddling too. But tonight he was paying to be debased and disciplined by someone so masterful that she expelled all thoughts of former mistresses from his mind. He was paying for an exorcism.

The room felt chillier when he was naked, and it made his cock hard. Degradation did it every time. He dropped to his knees and crossed the room on them, the merciless cement hinting at hardships to come. Once in front of her, he kept his eyes obediently on the floor.

"Get up and put your hands behind your back."

From the shadows she brought forward a table of implements. He tried to identify them in the diffused streetlight and she said, "Eyes on the ground," in that same authoritative voice. He obeyed.

Sofia walked behind him. A moment later, soft black leather cuffs enclosed his wrists. With the click of the lock, his stiff cock began to ache. Working with easy proficiency, she bound him from his hands to his biceps in a black leather arm-binder.

She stepped back and regarded her work. "Not bad. You would look even better with your legs trussed apart, but we need you mobile tonight."

Mobile. That said he was going to be put through his paces. Sofia inspected him with detached interest, pinching his nipples and tugging lightly on his balls. "So you're the man who lost his mistress. And now you're heartbroken. What was it about you that made her want to leave?"

"I don't know."

"Well, what was it about you that should have made her stay?"

"I—" And there it was, that unanswerable question: why would any mistress love him? "I don't know."

She snorted. "A self-aware sub is a joy indeed." She stroked his cock. "At least this is a decent size."

His blood surged. Kendall never handled his cock. He snuck a look at Sofia, who he could see now was somewhat petite even in those black boots, and had light stretch marks on her stomach. She was pretty, and her black, long-lashed eyes were mesmerizing, but overall she was hardly a goddess of perfection as Kendall always presented herself. And yet she didn't seem concerned in the least about her stretch marks or her nakedness or her slight pooch of a stomach. It was as if he was no more than a toy or a piece of furniture.

"Go stand in the corner."

"What?"

"Don't question me." She slapped his mouth, lightly. "I was hoping not to gag you tonight, but apparently you haven't been adequately trained."

She slipped a rubber ball into his mouth, the kind dogs chased for fun. "Now go stand in that corner. Don't make a sound until I summon you. And if that ball falls out of your mouth, the session ends immediately."

He shuffled into a corner so far from the ambient streetlight that he felt invisible. Nevertheless he stood obediently at attention, a submissive soldier waiting to be of service.

Sofia yawned and stretched her arms over her head. She was

easily the most confident, self-possessed woman he'd ever met, naked or clothed. She was looking through the table of implements—which he still couldn't view from his dark corner—when the door opened and a woman in a black tank top and jeans entered, her blonde hair in a ponytail. She paused with obvious hesitation.

Sofia snapped her fingers. "You're going to have a long night. Get started."

Kendall walked into the spill of streetlight.

Nate stifled a choking noise. This couldn't be possible. He was paying well, sure, but Kendall wasn't a pro domme. In fact, she sneered at the idea of anyone earning her favors other than through her whims. *I can't be bought*, she'd reminded him more than once. Yet here she was, stepping out of her heels and pulling off her tank top, then timidly reaching behind her to unhook her bra.

She nervously looked around the empty gas station as she slipped down her jeans and panties. She hadn't spotted him yet in the shadows. His teeth clenched around the dog ball. Seven months he'd spent in her service and not once had he seen her naked. Her small breasts and narrow back seemed unexpectedly frail.

A mix of pity and arousal went through him as she knelt on the chilly floor and looked up at Sofia.

"Why are you here?" Sofia asked.

"To serve you."

"Serve me how?"

"However you need. I'm your dog." Kendall bent over and kissed Sofia's boots.

His mind reeled. He'd always imagined Kendall imperious 24/7, whether dealing with waiters, ordering new shoes online or paying her water bill. But Sofia snapped a metal collar around

Kendall's slender neck and confirmed the unimaginable reality: Kendall was a switch. He wondered how long she'd been serving Sofia. Obviously she'd confided in her about their relationship, or Sofia wouldn't have known to set up this scene.

Sofia threw something across the room and said, "Get it." Kendall scuttled across the cement on all fours, picked it up in her mouth and returned with it. A leash, of course. She'd done that same trick to him, spanking him when he didn't move fast enough to fetch it or, god forbid, dropped it from his teeth.

"Good puppy," Sofia said, stroking Kendall's cheek. "Now bark like a dog for me."

Nate held his breath. His poised goddess would never bark like a dog. But she did it; his beautiful mistress began to bark while naked on all fours, a scenario so ludicrous and undignified that he knew he would never jerk off to thoughts of her again. Her mystique was evaporating by the second, but he barely cared because his cock was harder than ever at seeing this incredible and shocking performance. He wanted Sofia to show him every part of Kendall's body. He wanted Sofia to keep topping her, topping them both, commanding them to serve her and fuck her and adore her.

Sofia took Kendall's chin in hand. "You're going to do whatever I say tonight, just as a loyal and obedient little dog does. Right?"

Kendall nodded. He could only see her ponytail moving up and down, but he could imagine the pleasure—or fear, or both—in her eyes.

"Good girl. Get on the table."

Kendall climbed up on the long black table and opened her legs, looking like a naked buffet. Sofia tied her arms and feet to the table with effortless knot work. *Tie me up*, he thought. *Bind me, use me, make me your slave.*

Kendall was fully bound now, legs open. Sofia walked around her, idly pinching her nipples and flicking her clit. Kendall whimpered, a noise Nate had never heard her make but which seemed to be her version of a plea.

Sofia turned, her black eyes piercing the corner where he stood. "Come here," she commanded. "And drop the ball."

Nate's stomach lurched with excitement. What was happening seemed like an impossible dream as he walked toward the table. When Kendall saw him, she went very still. She looked at Sofia in confusion.

"Surprise," Sofia said, tickling her clit. She looked at Nate as he let the dog ball drop from his mouth. "You've always wanted to fuck her, haven't you?"

He nodded. "Yes, Mistress."

"Which Mistress?" she asked with a mean smile, taking hold of his cock.

"You. You are my only Mistress." The only mistress in the room, in his opinion.

She rolled a condom over his cock, palming him before dropping his shaft. Swiftly she undid his arm-binder. "Give me a show. Both of you. And make it hot or you'll both get the switch."

He searched Kendall's face for a hint of reluctance as he mounted her on the table, but her pale eyes were dazed with bliss. Hesitantly he ran his fingertips over her tits. She felt like a stranger, no relation to the cool and disdainful mistress he'd fucked so many times in his mind. She was simply Sofia's pet, a proxy he could use to impress. He sucked her nipples, but when Sofia sighed with boredom, he quickly moved between Kendall's legs.

His eyes had adjusted to the dimness now and with her legs tied apart, every detail of her pussy was exposed. He swallowed and slid two fingers inside her. A creamy heat enclosed them and she twisted on the table, whimpering again. He didn't know if Kendall was this wet and horny for him or for the perverse thrill of obeying Sofia, who watched them without expression. He didn't care. He was going to demonstrate exactly why any mistress should want to keep him.

He fingered her pussy and another soft little moan escaped Kendall. Sofia laughed. "Something you want to say, Kendall?"

"Please," Kendall whispered, her cheeks visibly coloring even in the dim light. "Fuck me. Please, Nate."

He positioned his cock against her slit and drove all of the way inside her. She felt as tight and smooth as he'd always dreamed, and he reminded himself that this was Kendall, his mistress, who'd dominated his dick and his brain for months. But now that he was fucking her, and she was twisting eagerly against her ropes, he could only think about pleasing Sofia. About showing off his endurance to her, the skills of his hips and the control of his cock—and the possibility that she might, someday, be his mistress, rather than his pro domme. That she might snap that metal collar around his neck and claim him as hers.

Sofia stalked around the table, cropping them lightly and warning them away from imaginary infractions, but he listened to her every word, more in tune with her commands than Kendall's cries. His balls were tight and his entire body ached to unload inside Kendall, but he wouldn't come until Sofia said so.

Kendall arched her back, moaning in gratitude for each thrust of his dick. Their stomachs were slapping together and a fiery brightness was ascending from his balls to his spine when Sofia dropped her crop.

"You two do look good together," she mused.

Nimbly she climbed onto the table and settled herself on Kendall's mouth, facing Nate. Reaching between her legs, she lifted her clitoral hood as Kendall's tongue disappeared inside her pussy.

Nate leaned over Kendall, her sweat-dampened chest clinging to his, and licked Sofia's clit. She squeezed her breasts and undulated on Kendall's mouth like a snake. It was everything he'd ever wanted and never expected to get, a domme naked and moaning on his face as she exploited all of his submissive desires. Sofia rode both of their mouths now, pushing her salty heat onto their tongues without shame as they licked and sucked her as artfully as they could. Kendall's pussy was quivering around his dick and she felt like his twin, his female half dedicated to the art of worshiping the feminine supreme.

Sofia's body tensed and a brief, broken cry escaped her; then she ejaculated over both of their faces, thrusting slippery and wet against their mouths in the throes of her orgasm. The euphoria of satisfying his goddess rocketed through Nate and he came with white-hot joy, his balls tingling as Kendall's pussy squeezed around him in her own orgasm.

Sofia caught her breath and climbed off the table, dismounting gracefully in her black boots. Her long, dark hair clung to her cheeks and she pushed it back with a shaky smile. She rumpled Nate's hair.

"Not bad," she said. "Who knows? You might get a collar yet."

"Did you know?" he asked Patrick.

It was Tuesday. They were in their neighborhood bar, but the crack of the balls on the pool table and the amber ceiling lights seemed muted, as in a dream. His mind was still riveted on last Friday night.

"I heard rumors," Patrick shrugged.

Nate integrated that. "You could have told me," he said finally.

"And kill your boner? You never would have been happy with Kendall if you knew she was a switch. If you knew she was someone's dog." Patrick snickered.

Nate drank his beer.

"Look, did it work at least?" Patrick asked. "The 'exorcism'?"

"In part." Nate looked out the window of the bar. "It was more of a transference, really." He unconsciously touched his neck, imagining the metal collar around his throat.

BUSINESS MANAGING

Teresa Noelle Roberts

How many times do I have to tell you that a scribbled note on a stained napkin isn't a receipt?" The strained patience in Ms. Bridges's voice stroked Dan's cock.

He shrugged, acting like the slightly flaky entrepreneur that he sometimes was, talking to his long-suffering business manager. "I'm sorry. I forgot to get one when we ordered and by the time I stopped back, the truck had moved."

Dan's business was fair-trade, organic specialty products: coffee, chocolate, spices, sauces. Ms. Bridges's business was keeping Dan organized so he could focus on the parts of the job he loved: traveling to exotic places and working directly with farmers and artisanal producers, helping them get better lives for their families at the same time he got delicious products for his customers.

At least that was what he'd hired Ms. Bridges to do. At the final interview, he'd explained he needed someone tough minded and detail oriented to keep him in line. "I'm creative and very passionate," he'd explained, "but I need someone to keep me disciplined." He'd meant he needed someone who'd keep him on track about the myriad details of running a small business, which he tended to neglect in favor of the fun parts. As soon as he said the words, though, he realized he'd been looking at the tall, lean blonde in a suit too severe for his casual office and fantasizing about needing her discipline in areas other than keeping tax paperwork organized. He felt his face blaze, hoping it was hidden under the tan of his recent trip to Central America. Maybe, he hoped, he hadn't made a complete ass of himself and offended the best candidate for a business manager he'd interviewed yet.

Somehow the devil had been on his side that day. She'd smiled in a way that lit her somewhat austere face and said, "I think that would be a pleasure, in every sense of the word."

Dan might own the company, but the business manager was the real boss—especially after hours, when they were alone in the office. And right now, the business manager had some pointed questions.

"Why in the world are you taking a supermarket buyer to lunch at a taco truck anyway?" This time he read amusement under the cool façade. Good. It wouldn't do to actually piss off Ms. Bridges—her name was Melanie, but she insisted on being called Ms. Bridges, like a much older woman might. Annoyed, she'd just keep up the dealing-with-the-idiot-boss routine. That would be no fun for either of them. If he amused and aggravated her in equal measure, though, things would be different, and much, much better.

Dan broke into a grin. "If he didn't appreciate Juan's Tacos, there was no way he'd appreciate what we're doing here. People have to see more than the bottom line, because our products cost a bit more than mass-produced crap. They have to understand flavor, and get that handmade with love *should* cost a little more, and that flavor matters more than glossy packaging. Juan makes the best tacos in town."

"Point." Ms. Bridges stood and leaned forward over the big executive desk. He'd bought it for himself originally, but found a battered nineteenth-century kitchen table, scarred by generations of long-dead cooks suited his style much better—and the classic executive desk suited Ms. Bridges. The stretch across the expanse of cool steel accented the long, slender lines of her body and suggested a cleavage view that her serious, round-necked knit top didn't allow. "But take people for tacos *after* you've sealed the deal, and get a receipt when you do—in English, and not on a napkin."

Dan's cock jumped at the vehemence in her voice. She was controlled, but there was fire under the control, and he'd learned to trace its flickerings in the most mundane moments. There was a hint of a smile in her eyes, not echoed in the stern set of her lips.

Perfect.

Now would be the time to tell her. "I sealed the deal. He said his mind was made up, while he was still here, tasting the coffee and the new chocolate line, and seeing how well you had the business side of things under control."

Ms. Bridges smiled at him in that special way that let him know under the cool façade she was just as excited as he was. "Congratulations. You worked hard on that deal and listened to me when I had to rein you in and keep you focused on it instead of tilting at fifty-seven windmills. I'm proud of you, Dan. That deserves a reward." She half crawled onto the desk to kiss him, looking like some great, predatory cat. His head swam at the taste of her lipstick, at the hint of orange chocolate on her breath—on the simple closeness after a few long days when they were too busy with work to acknowledge the other side of their relationship.

She pulled back long before Dan wanted, but he knew better than to hold her when she was ready to go. "On the other hand, there was the matter of the receipt, and the fact you still haven't returned a potentially important call from Monday—I know because she called again today—so there will be punishment as well as reward."

Ms. Bridges settled back in her chair as if nothing unusual had been said or done.

He shivered with anticipation. Her rare rewards were extremely motivational. Then again, her punishments were at least as delicious.

But this one could be bad. The receipt was nothing and they both knew it, the kind of thing he'd do deliberately just to give her a reason to spank him. But not returning that particular call was another story. "I'd been putting off calling the woman from Whole Foods back until I was done with the Hannaford meeting. Truth is, we can work with a regional supermarket chain like Hannaford now, but we're not ready to go national. We don't have the supply chain in place yet, and I can only build that chain one village co-op at a time. And I was afraid…"

"You were afraid you'd get too excited and make a commitment you couldn't meet if you didn't take the time to think it through. That makes sense, but Dan, you should have had me call back and set up a call later in the week when you could focus, not leave her hanging."

Dan nodded, his excitement and his cock both sinking. Ms. Bridges was right, of course. The Whole Foods buyer would understand if he set up a call for a mutually convenient time but wouldn't understand being blown off. He might not be ready to work with Whole Foods yet, but he'd hate to burn any bridges.

"Do you think she'd believe me if I said I'd been in Columbia or something?"

Ms. Bridges smiled rather evilly. "I said Indonesia, since you were there last week, in case she asked questions. I figured the time difference was enough you'd have an excuse for not calling on your cell. But you owe me."

"Extra vacation day?" he said hopefully, knowing that while she might take him up on it, it wouldn't save him.

"I was thinking more like ten stripes, and lines. Definitely lines."

He knew he shouldn't bargain, but damn it, lines were a waste of time. "Twenty stripes and no lines?" He couldn't help himself. He grinned as he said it, although he knew it was probably the last thing he should do.

"Fifteen stripes and lines. I'm not a cocoa producer who expects you to bargain for the best price." Now he'd done it. He winced, thinking of how sore his ass would be by the time she was done with him, and how much time tonight he'd waste writing lines. At the same time, his cock was stirring, stretching, hardening at the thought. It would hurt. He knew it would hurt.

It would hurt wonderfully.

And he needed to learn to be more organized and responsible if the business was going to succeed, so the lines were a wise idea as well. He hated lines, but they always seemed to work to remind him not to screw up whatever he'd screwed up.

And he needed to learn to obey Ms. Bridges without question.

"Position!" Ms. Bridges said sharply.

Dan scrambled to his feet and dropped his pants without delay, kicking off his shoes as the pants crumbled around his ankles. Resisting the temptation to simply kick pants and shoes aside, he folded the pants over the arm of his chair and set the shoes neatly next to it, as Ms. Bridges would want. He wasn't wearing underwear. It made life easier if he didn't, with the amount of time he ended up over Ms. Bridges's knee, or bent over her desk.

He leaned forward, bracing his hands on the cool edge of the desk. His whole body clenched into a knot of anticipation, half fear and half wicked excitement. It was barely six and it was possible someone else from their small staff was still in the office. That made the surge of terror and desire stronger, knowing the edge they walked. Ms. Bridges usually waited until later, when she was sure they were alone. If she was going to work him over now, he must really deserve it.

And she must really need it, as badly as he did. That thought stiffened his cock as much as anything else. Dan knew he needed her, craved her like coffee and chocolate, but she rarely let him know she needed a sub to torment and mold as much as he needed to be tormented and molded. Part of her game was to pretend it was all in a day's work.

She unlocked the top drawer of the desk and took out a small, slender fiberglass wand, almost like a conductor's baton. There was no room to stash a classic cane in the office, but this little toy more than did the trick.

Dan closed his eyes and followed the sound of her movements: the click of her high heels on the wood floor behind the desk, and the shush of her skirts, astonishingly loud in the quiet. The only thing louder was the rush of his own blood, the pounding of his heart. It was only a few steps around the desk, but it took a lifetime for her to take them.

"Count, Dan," she said, her voice coming from behind him, stern but not unkind, like a kindergarten teacher keeping a child in line.

Fire slashed across his ass. "One," he counted, managing not
to shriek by sheer force of will. He'd wind up yelling and whimpering, but Ms. Bridges liked him to start out tough.

It gave her something to break, and he liked the feeling of
being broken.

Sometimes she gave him time between strokes to reach the
point that pain seared into pleasure. Not this time. The fierce
little baton cracked down again, laying a line parallel to the first
one. "Two." Three, four, five and six came in rapid succession,
too fast to process. His voice was still steady as he counted,
but his cock wasn't steady at all. It fell with the sharp pain of
each blow, but started to bounce back in the seconds before she
struck again. The pleasurable kind of pain was just out of reach.
His cock knew it, even if his brain and his abused butt weren't
so sure. He flinched away instinctively, then equally instinctively
pushed back to catch the next stroke.

She paused between six and seven, and again between seven
and eight, giving him time to catch up, to feel the hot pain trans-
mute to hot joy, spreading out from the tender stripes on his ass
and sliding through his whole body.

Eight was harder than the others, jolting him so the number
became a cry of pain. At the same time, the shock of pain filled
his bones with heat and his cock with blood, while it emptied
his brain of fear.

He hadn't known how nervous he'd been about the meeting
today, how anxious he still was about the big commitment he'd
made on behalf of his little company. Ms. Bridges's caning was
taking him away from that place of anxiety to a place where
nothing mattered except sensation and need, except pain and
lust, except Ms. Bridges and pleasing her.

The next few blows were harder yet, cutting through all his
defense. He managed to get the numbers out, but even to his

own ears, they seemed less and less intelligible, more like incoherent snarls. He didn't pull away, though every muscle and nerve screamed for him to do so. She trusted him to hold still when she beat him, so he would, dammit.

His brain slipped away. The baton struck again, and he thought it was just as hard as before, but all he could feel was heat, overwhelming his reason and hardening his cock unbearably. "Twelve," he gasped. "No...eleven."

"Good boy, Dan." A small, cool hand stroked his hot ass, soothing and enflaming him simultaneously. "Honest even when it would be to your benefit not to be. Do you want me to go easy on you with the last four?"

His muddled mind would have had trouble coming up with an answer to most questions, but this one was easy. "Only if you want to." He wasn't sure if he hoped she'd go easy or she wouldn't.

She didn't, but she murmured, "Good boy; good, brave boy," with each strike and so the pain didn't matter. He soared on it, rode it to a place above his own body where he could gaze at Ms. Bridges's terrible beauty, even though in the real world he was facing away from her. Time blurred. He was counting because she'd told him to, but he didn't know what the numbers meant anymore; he only knew she wanted them.

The fifteenth blow felt like a knife slicing into his flesh, slicing away everything unnecessary. He sobbed out the number, unashamed of the tears he couldn't control.

Ms. Bridges did something then she didn't often do: she helped him stand, turning him slightly as she did, then put her arms around him and drew him close. She never left him alone at the end of a session to put himself back together. She'd stay in contact, one hand on his shoulder or thigh, but she rarely cuddled like this. Through the blur of tears and the bigger blur of endorphins, Dan drank in her smile, her touch. "I'm proud of you, Dan. Proud of how you took that, but also proud of where you're taking the company. We're on the verge of something big."

"Couldn't have done it without you." His words slurred like he was an old drunk. "That's why...I'm gonna make you a partner."

She silenced him with a kiss that somehow managed to be both passionate and protective. He hesitated for a second and then dared to kiss her back. Her lips were sweeter and richer and more complex than the chocolate he got from that little village in Mexico, the coarse-textured stone-ground stuff with a touch of chili along with vanilla and dark pilon sugar. He groaned into her mouth. With his last reserves of will, he managed not to pump his straining cock against her—an effort that she subverted by grinding against him.

"I'm serious about the partnership," he continued when she moved away from his mouth. "You deserve it."

"I probably do—and I definitely like the idea. But you have about four brain cells left and they're all saying, 'Whee!' so we'll talk about it tomorrow. Right now, I want your cock."

Dan gaped. They'd fucked a few times, always at her whim, but it was such a rarity he'd almost given up yearning for it, hoping for it.

Almost. He was only human.

"I told you that you deserve a reward. Lie down, Dan." The carpet was thin and the floor was hard, but, drunk on endorphins and anticipation, Dan didn't care. She tossed a condom packet onto his stomach and he scrambled to put it on, watching her undress as he did. He didn't get to do that nearly often enough, but he suspected it would never get old.

Ms. Bridges undressed as efficiently as she did everything

else, placing her clothes neatly over her chair. Under her sweater and skirt, she wore sheer gray stockings, a red garter belt and a pair of tiny red panties that she slipped off without disturbing the garter belt. A red lacy bra that accented her breasts more than it hid them completed the look. She caught him gaping like a cartoon character, shrugged, and said, "Some things become clichés because they work."

He made a strangled noise of affirmation. He'd intended words to be involved, but at that moment, she crouched down over him and words failed. "I'm going to ride you hard," she whispered, her voice husky with need under a façade of pretend-cool. "But don't you dare come until I say you can."

The authority in her words pushed him closer to the edge, and the feel of her cunt pushed him even closer, hot and tight and slick as she engulfed him. She let out a soft moan, sounding almost surprised by her own pleasure. Dan froze, already hovering near the precipice of orgasm, afraid to move lest he fall over. "Touch me," she snarled, and his hands moved to obey while his brain focused desperately on not coming.

He could only think about Central American politics, coffee roasts and the fact they needed to hire someone to deal with social media for so long, though, with Ms. Bridges's clit slick under his fingers, Ms. Bridges's cunt gripping him, Ms. Bridges riding him hard, Ms. Bridges's stripes on his ass getting abraded against the carpet from the force of her fucking, the pain adding to the pleasure. Her abs were quivering already—she'd gotten worked up from the beating, as much as he had. She leaned forward, pressing herself against his hand, slamming onto his cock. The smell of female desire and his own heat combined deliciously with the ever-present coffee scent from the roasting room downstairs and he had the ridiculous thought that if he could make a specialty flavor of that combination, he'd become a rich man overnight. She was riding him, gripping him, controlling him; only he couldn't control himself much longer. His cock was twitching and bucking, and he wanted to obey, but his damn body had its own ideas and he didn't know if his will would contain his lust much longer.

Ms. Bridges laid one hand on his chest. "Breathe," she whispered. "I need you to hold on a little while longer. Just a little while." Her hand was cool and her voice was calm, but her cunt was hot and rippling and her eyes were wild, and it was obvious she was working as hard at containing herself as he was.

That made it easier to hold out. She wanted him to hold on, just a little while longer, so he would let go and follow her will. Simple as that. He breathed deeply, concentrated on her face rather than the movements of her body and the grip of her sex. His cock throbbed as wildly as ever, but he detached himself from it, focusing on the woman who rode him, on her pleasure rather than his own. It wasn't long before her muscles locked and she exclaimed harshly, "Now, Dan."

He let go everything he'd been holding in check, gripping her hips and pumping up into her. She cried out again, convulsing hard around him, then collapsed forward onto his chest. "Come," she said, her voice a little dazed, but still commanding.

He released in a hot explosion that burned away all the residual stresses of the week.

Ms. Bridges kissed him on the forehead before she stood and began cleaning herself up. Even if she'd been a snuggly person the office floor wasn't exactly comfortable. Now that his sexual high was subsiding, Dan was noticing just how scratchy the carpet was, especially on his butt, which now probably had rug burns on top of the stripes.

It wasn't until they were both dressed and semicomposed that Ms. Bridges said, "About those lines…"

Dan's face fell. He knew better than to beg, but damn, he'd hoped the heat of sex had burned the lines right out of her brain—even though he knew all too well that she forgot nothing.

"I'd been thinking about 'I will remember to get receipts,' or 'I will always return phone calls promptly, if only to set up a better time to talk.' But I think, 'I will talk to my business manager if I'm getting overwhelmed and need backup, because that's why I hired her in the first place' will do. One hundred times, best penmanship, on my desk tomorrow."

His hand ached just thinking about it, but he couldn't help grinning. She knew what he needed. "How about business partner? I have my pants on now, so we can talk about it."

She grinned back. "You entrepreneurial types can do what you want, but I don't like to talk business after hours. We'll talk about that in the morning—after you give me the lines."

A LITTLE
TICKLISH

Colin

She comes in with bare feet, and I'm tied down at just the right angle to the door so that I can see them. She stands in the doorway for a good long while, giving me a good long look. Fresh red polish on her slim toes and a silver anklet. The rest of her is just as casual, there's nothing especially domme-like in tonight's outfit. Tonight she's all about blue jeans and baby-doll tees; this evening's selection is pink, with PRINCESS spelled on it in sequins. It's her feet that catch my eye and hold it. She smirks as she ventures into the playroom. When she leans against the table she makes a thing of kicking one foot up behind her (I can see her sole, long, with those deep wrinkles), then catching it in her hand and pulling it toward her ass, like stretching before a run. Wriggling her long toes, clenching them like fingers. But I know why she's doing it.

"I am going to tickle the living crap out of you tonight," she tells me, her voice low and somehow confidential, like this is a little piece of intel she wants to get in before things properly begin. There's an edge of laughter in her voice too. This means she's turned on; silly as she thinks all this is, tonight she really *wants* to do it. Tonight she wants to see me squirm. I'm in trouble.

The knowledge makes me hard. It also freaks me out just a very little bit. She tied me down good, half an hour before, and then left me to stew, listening to *Carmina Burana* while she got her head ready for the scene. That's standard procedure. I *like* being tied up—usually. I like the blank, floaty feeling that comes after a while when you've held your stretched-out limbs perfectly still for a good long time. You can feel your head emptying out, all the poisons draining. It's bliss.

Usually.

Tonight, for some reason, it was hell. Maybe I picked up on whatever it was that had got her hot, but I was antsy from the first moment she tightened the straps. Sometimes the blank feeling doesn't come; instead there's a moment when you try to move your forearms and you can't. You don't panic, but you know nothing you do or say for the next hour or so is going to matter and you have to deal with that. Pure helplessness. It's exhilarating, in a way—this is what it's supposed to be about, after all. But you have to find a way to get inside your head fast or, seriously, you can go a little crazy.

So I concentrated on my standard images. Dentist chair stuff: flowers in warm breezes, mountain views.

But it didn't help much. And now that she's told me what she's got planned, suddenly I'm five years old again. *Omigod, omigod, she's going to do it to me. She's gonna get me.*

She might have used the flogger, the violet wand, the rosewood box of needles. She might even have used a feather or two in combination with the above, and I would have dealt with it. But she's going to *tickle* me. That's the main course. *Bon appétit*, baby.

"You ticklish?" she asks me, and she cracks her knuckles.

"Little," I whisper. "Little ticklish..."

She frowns, a hand at her ear. "What's that? I didn't hear you."

"Little..." I clear my throat. "I'm a little ticklish. Yeah."

"Yeah? Good. Good." She looks me over, planning her strategy. It's simultaneously flattering and terrifying. When she speaks again, I start violently.

"What's this? Huh?" Her hand with its red nails moves out to cover my navel, rotates its palm counterclockwise over the very tip-top of my belly hair. Just like that, we've begun.

"Don't..." I don't mean to say it. It slips out.

"Don't?" The hand stops. Her eyes—chocolate-brown eyes that go badly with her blonde hair, her fair and freckled skin—widen at me. "Did you just say 'Don't'?" She almost whispers it.

I lick my lips, shut my eyes tight. Battening down the hatches. The closest I can come to escaping. As bad a move, really, as if I'd spat in her face. I'm supposed to participate. If I weren't feeling so strange and squirmy, I would have. I'd have said, *That's my belly button.* Very respectfully.

And I really should have. I should have been a good little tickle-slave. Because that's the way you avoid the real torture—at least until she realizes she's being played.

But I say nothing and keep my eyes closed, even when she snaps her fingers under my nose.

"Somebody's being a little snot tonight."

Then her finger is drilling into the cup of my navel. She keeps her nails short, though polished, and the nail on her forefinger is right down to the nub. Even so, she's got me screaming in like five seconds. My feet are bad, there are places on my sides that will drive me fucking insane, but something about a finger in

my belly button—just diddling that little nub of flesh in there—
makes me lose it.

I laugh hard, pushing it out, trying to work with the tickling
instead of fighting it. If you do that, sometimes you can get past
it. But not tonight.

Tonight she owns me.

She's not just doing my navel; she's scratching lightly at my
sides, smiling sweetly down at me while I howl and gabble.

I have some idea what she's feeling, having been on the
other side of the cuffs before. There's something about tickling
someone who's tied up and completely helpless, their whole body
stretched out before you smorgasbord-wise. A little like playing
a keyboard. You never realized how inviting ribs and knees and
toes can be, especially when peals of laughter are the payoff. It's
a revelation how good it can be to just play with someone's body
when they can't do anything about it. Erotic? Oh yeah.

Then the game changes; she goes for my nipples, and that's
hell, that is fucking *agony*. She doesn't pinch; it'd be easier on
me if she did, the pain would give me something to focus on.
Instead she strokes, circles the areolae with her fingertips until
there are two hard and pricked-up points on my chest. Did I
mention that it was agony?

She giggles as she's doing it. Ticklish feet she understands;
ribs, even the navel. It's all basic stuff; she's not particularly
ticklish herself, but if you scratch her arches, say, she'll react.
Even giggle a little if you get her just right. But for some reason
my nipples have always struck her as just cute. Just funny. Play
with *her* tits and she melts; with her the sensation goes straight
to her pussy. But in her mind men don't work the same way. And
usually we don't, so how can I bitch?

My cock aches. Of course all this action has had a very
noticeable effect on it. I've been hard since she walked those

bare feet into the playroom, but now I'm rigid, so hard it hurts. I want her to stop screwing with my nipples and wrap her hand around my dick. Pull it. Stroke it. My balls are ticklish too, but I'd give anything for a little of *that* torture right now.

I try to get her attention, shaking my hips as best I can, but all that does is send my dick flopping from side to side. Not that it matters. She knows what I'm trying to do, and it's funny to her. She laughs at me.

"Uh-uh, baby. If someone were sweet before, I might have played with his winkie a little. Sure. But no, *somebody* was a little bitch, so no dice."

I try to play it the way she likes it, whining and whimpering—then begging her with Shakespearean eloquence. But as she said, it's too late for that. All my whining is another opportunity to put me in my place.

"You horny? Huh? Widdle baby wanna cum a big one?"

She rarely uses baby talk, except when she's tickling me. Something about it makes me laugh as well—I don't know what, it might just be a defense mechanism, because I hate baby talk, even when it's meant affectionately. She knows that, and so usually she uses it sparingly.

She's leading up to something.

Eventually she gets there. She climbs lightly up onto the table, graceful as a big blonde cat, and turns herself round to face my feet. The table is broad enough that she can do this without actually getting on top of me; there's just space enough on either side of my body for hers.

I can see her denim-sheathed ass and, most importantly, the soles of her own feet, which she's laid on my chest. She's wriggling her toes again, pinching one crab-wise between the first two toes of her other foot; teasing me.

A good scene will end with me worshipping her feet. But I

know we're nowhere near the end of this one. Because now she's playing with *my* feet. Sliding her fingers over them, caressing my ankles and plucking at my toes. Tickling them. And now we're in a whole new circle of hell.

For a guy—so I'm told—I have nice feet. I make sure I keep them well-groomed for her. Here's the thing about them: they're not as bad a spot for tickling as my navel or my nipples; you couldn't really torture information out of me using my feet, the way you could using those other places. But once you get me laughing by tickling my feet, it's a low, steady roaring that will not quit. Once I get started, it takes very little effort to keep me howling—just a little *kitchy* here, a little *koo* there. And it excites me far more than if you tickle even my balls—some kind of by-product of my own foot fetish, probably.

So now I'm burning, my cock hard against my belly. Helpless. All I can do is lie there laughing, watching her feet rub slowly against each other. I can't see where on my soles she's going to strike next. She teases me with her feet, until I'm begging for them. I don't even care if she keeps tickling me. All I want is those toes in my mouth.

Every now and then her hand reaches behind her for my cock and strokes it just a little, like she's taking time out to remind herself I have more parts. Expanding her horizons, as you might say.

"I told you I was gonna tickle the crap out of you," she tells me, purring it. "Didn't I? You want my tootsies?" She stretches a leg, and her cold toes are bunched against my lips, a bundle too firmly packed for me to kiss or suck them. Then, just as quickly, they're gone.

I do want those feet. I tell her so. I beg her for them. But I know I'm not getting them anytime soon. Tomorrow's Saturday, after all. We could go all night. Eventually she'll untie me and give me a sweet, drawn-out blow job, or climb on me and fuck me, if she's really excited. But that's not going to be for a while yet, and it'll be a long, laughing time before I taste her toes. You want to know the really funny thing? She hates her feet. Thinks they're ugly and disgusting. She says she can't understand why I love them so damned much, and yet the fact that I do has eroticized them for her. She gets pedicures, has a rainbow's worth of colored nail polishes, and creams and lotions enough to drown you. No matter how much she sneers, she wants them to smell good, look good and feel good.

So, when she finally does give them to me, it'll be with this shuddery, sexy smile, lips stretched tight to keep the laughter in. She's never talked to me about how she feels during those moments, but I imagine she feels small and laughable, embarrassed as hell—but also exultant. Like she's burning up inside with white fire.

And you know what?

I can relate.

HOUND
AND HARE

D. L. King

So, you're a hasher. You're a runner? You run races? I mean, that's cool."

I met him in a downtown bar. I was there for a porn-film release party. He was there with his running group.

"Not exactly," he said.

"C L!" One of his buddies gave him the thumbs-up salute as he left the bar. He saluted back with a raised glass.

"So, your name's C L?"

"Tom," he said. "Hashing isn't racing. It's just for fun. It's an international runners club that got its start in the British Army back in the thirties. It's about beer and running. Like, running for beer. Like, we have this slogan: Drinkers with a running problem. Uh." He took a draft from his pint and explained the concept to me.

Evidently, it's a hounds and hare thing. Someone is the hare and that person sets the course. He (or she) lays down marks and signs for the runners, or the hounds, to follow. The course doesn't follow any reasonable route to get from the start to the finish—where there's always beer. It can go through buildings, across playgrounds; it usually doubles back on itself a few times. That's here in New York. If you were running in, say, Florida, the course might take you through town to the beach and double back, leading you through a muddy swamp before you ended up at the beer. The course is usually several miles and takes a few hours to complete, much of that time put to use trying to find the next sign and drinking beer in pubs it might lead you through along the way.

The trail is marked with chalk or charcoal or flour, something that isn't permanent. The marks might be on the sidewalk, the sides of buildings, the street, streetlamps, anywhere—and god help you if it rains and washes away a lot of the signs. Sometimes people run in costumes. Some places, where they can do it without getting arrested, they might even run naked. It's kind of a big moving party.

"Sounds like fun," I said. But, if you're name's Tom, why did that guy call you C L?"

"Oh, that's my hasher name."

A woman in hot-pink running shorts and a black tank top with a graphic of a box of Trojan condoms and a slogan under it that said BE PREPARED, wandered past. She was drinking a pint of something light. When she got close, she caught Tom's eye and, with her free hand, she pulled her shirt and part of her racing bra down to expose one of her breasts. She readjusted her clothing and then made the universal, *I'm watching you* sign, with two fingers, before moving on.

"That your girlfriend?"

"Nah, she's just a friend."

"So, C L, huh? What's it stand for?" I asked.

"Well, so, uh, one day I was running in running shorts that

were really loose and short, uh, without a jock. And, I guess my
junk kinda spilled out, you know? So, at the end of the run I got
my hasher name. Someone said, 'Someone oughta lock that shit
up,' so—I am now and forever Cocky Locky."

He looked slightly embarrassed, but then he gave me this
glorious smile. So—not too embarrassed. "Ever had it locked
up?" He looked at me and then down, and smiled again. "Want
to?" He took a drink of beer. "I'd be happy to lock it up for
you."

Another beer on his part, and another vodka on mine, and I
suggested he follow me home. He seemed happy to comply.

We got to know each other over the next few weeks. It actually
wasn't until our second date that I actually locked his cock up.
The first night was spent exploring each other's body; learning
what was a turn-on and what was a turn-off. He learned that I
liked receiving head, and I learned that he liked having his balls
fondled. He even liked it a little rough, which I found absolutely charming. He also found that my discovering he liked
rough handling was a great turn-on for me. He liked having
his nipples bitten. That alone produced copious amounts of
precome. And, though he was shy about it and sort of shocked
when I first did it, he seemed to enjoy having me play with
his ass.

Of course, I knew what turned me on, but watching him
discover it, and discover it also turned him on, seemed to be
something very new for him. I suppose he'd been happy fucking
the random girl, or being in vanilla relationships before.
Somehow, he'd never realized what he really wanted—or maybe
he had, but had never had the opportunity to act on it. So, my
taking control ended up being a revelation for him.

Being a runner, Tom had a great body. Nice, compact,

tight ass, concave on the sides; long, sinewy, muscular legs; long, thin fingers and pretty feet. He was strong and wiry with short brown hair and hooded dark-brown eyes, which I found *über* sexy. On our second date, we met for Chinese food at a place close to the bar. From there, we went to another bar to hear a local band that seemed poised to become the next big thing. And then, since he seemed up for it and was reasonably well lubricated, I dragged him to my lair to do, or at least suggest, all manner of evil things to him.

I live on the Lower East Side, in a fifth-floor walk-up apartment. It was really close to the bar we'd just vacated, but it's that five-story climb that will get you, especially if you aren't used to it. Being a runner, Tom managed it pretty well but was more winded than I by the time he made it to the top. Once inside the apartment, I pushed him down on the couch and stripped him, telling him he'd cool off faster that way. And anyway, I enjoyed running my hands through the sweat on his chest.

I pulled off his jeans and underwear—lime green: cool—and then watched his cock as I stood and slowly stripped down to bra and panties. He seemed to appreciate the sheer black lace covering my tits and pussy. I put a hand on his cock, teasing it with my fingertips, backed up and led him to the bedroom.

Pushing him down on the bed, I climbed on top and ground, full length, against him, initiating a deep kiss. I snaked my hand underneath my body and wrapped it around his hard cock, pulling and stretching it between us. He groaned into my mouth and grabbed my ass, pushing me tighter to him.

"Do you know what BDSM is?" I asked him, licking and scraping my teeth over his nipples.

"Sure, I've seen it on the Internet. Why? Do you want me to do that stuff to you; tie you up and stuff?"

"No, Tom," I said. I bit down on his nipple and he arched his back, pushing his groin against me and groaning. I smiled at him. "No, sweetie. I'm going to do that stuff to you." I felt his cock jump against me as I pushed him back against the bed.

"But I never did—I mean, I don't think…"

"Relax C L, you'll love it," I said, pushing myself into a sitting position atop his hips and toying with his cock. I held it against my lace-covered cunt and rubbed it against myself.

That night I introduced him to a few toys: clothespins for his nipples, which turned his cock into a leaky faucet; a padded leather paddle for his perfect runner's butt, which pinked up nicely with a few gentle swats, and a blindfold for sex. The blindfold seemed to make the biggest impression on him. Bigger, even, than the clothespins.

I tied his wrists to the bed with scarves, figuring I'd save the actual leather cuffs until he was a bit more comfortable with the whole idea. Once his hands were immobilized, I introduced the blindfold. His breathing sped and his head snapped to me every time I moved or made a sound. He jumped when I scratched at his nipples with my fingernails and jumped again when I lowered my mouth to his cock and swirled my tongue around its head. When I pulled on his balls he moaned and pushed his groin into my hands.

"Oh, you like that, do you?" I gently smacked his cock with my free hand. He sucked in a breath and his cock jerked but stayed hard. I smacked it a little harder, fascinated to see how his body would react.

"Mother fucker," he yelled, but thrust himself toward me at the same time. He bit his upper lip.

"Like that, too, huh?" I asked. I lowered my mouth to him again. Again, he jumped but then relaxed.

"Jesus Christ, this is fucking unreal," he said.

"Oh, honey, this is nothing. Just you wait," I said, pulling the blindfold off. "I have such plans for you." Without untying his wrists, I smoothed a condom on him and pushed my panties to the side as I slid onto him, taking him in to the root, grinding hard against him.

The sex, while short, was good. I knew he wouldn't be able to last very long after my getting him that excited, but that was all right; we'd work on it. I left him tied to the bed while I removed the filled condom and cleaned him up. "Are you seeing anyone," I asked.

"No," he said. "Just you, if you want to."

"When's your next run?"

"Saturday afternoon. Why?"

It was Thursday. Who knew if either of us would be any good at work tomorrow, but who cared, really? It would be Friday, anyway. I got off the bed and went over to the dresser to retrieve a box. "I have a present for you," I said, opening the box and taking out the chastity device. Before he could say anything, or see what I held, I snapped it onto his now-flaccid cock and balls. I closed the little plastic lock and showed him the key, which I put inside a little ornate box on the bedside table.

"I told you I'd lock it up for you. By the way, I never got to come. Do you think that's right? You think it's right that you get to come, and I don't?"

His mouth formed an O. "Oh, shit. Sorry! I didn't mean to, um, you want me to, I mean I could eat you, or something." He grinned his best cute-little-boy grin and cocked his head. "You want to untie my hands?"

"No, that's Okay." I leaned back away from him and took my bra off, then removed my panties. "I can do it." On my knees, between his legs, I began to masturbate. I was already wet from our earlier games and from putting him in chastity, so my finger slipped inside easily. I pumped it in and out a few times before adding a second finger, pumping them both more vigorously, making that wet, sucking, slurping sound.

He pulled his knees up and humped the air. Unfortunately, there was no way for him to get hard while wearing the device. In fact, the act of arousal was a bit painful, I would imagine. I could tell he wanted to touch himself, but his hands were restrained. And, of course, I knew that even if he'd had use of them, it wouldn't have done him any good. The device wouldn't allow his fingers inside. He was locked up tight, but he'd easily be able to bathe and attend to business, although peeing would be much easier and far less messy sitting down. Ah, well, he'd find that out on his own. Just the thought made me squeeze my breast and pinch the nipple before bringing the hand down to circle my clit while the other hand pumped inside. The more I thought about his arousal, the louder the little obscene noises coming from my pussy got. The louder the noises got, the more tortured he looked, poor baby. When he gave a strangled cry, I came. It was a nice, long orgasm with lots of little after-quakes; just the release I needed.

I removed my fingers from my cunt and held them under his nose before pushing them into his mouth. He closed his eyes and sucked on them, wrapping his tongue between and around them, cleaning every little bit of come off them before I withdrew them and untied his wrists.

"Wow, that was fucking amazing," he said. He reached between his legs to explore the device attached to his genitals. "Mind if I look?" he asked.

"Of course not, be my guest," I replied, smiling.

He jumped off the bed and walked over to the full-length mirror by my closet. He turned this way and that and humped the air, looking at the chastity cage. He ran his fingers over it again and whistled. "That's pretty cool." He looked up and smiled at me. "So, Okay, take it off."

"No, Cocky Locky. You'll remain locked up all tomorrow and through the run on Saturday. That way, you can be sure that your *junk* won't fall out of your shorts again."

"But, I don't wear those shorts anymore," he said.

"Be that as it may, you're going to remain locked up until I release you. You can call me from the bar, at the end of the run, and I'll meet you there. Does that sound good?" He gave me a look. "Well, whatever. It won't come off until Saturday—*if* I take it off then. We'll see." He gasped. "Here," I handed him his underwear and pants. "Put these on."

Looking at me the whole time, he stepped into his underwear and gingerly pulled them up, then did the same with his jeans. When he was dressed, I put my clothes back on, too.

"See, no one can tell you're wearing it. You'll be fine." I stepped in for a kiss and grabbed his ass, shoving myself against his crotch. "Call me tomorrow night, after work." With a final kiss, I let him out the door. "Get home safe," I said.

That night I thought of all the fun we could have. We could have our own hash, maybe a sort of scavenger-hunt hash. I could set the trail with lots of stops along the way for him to pick up little fun items, or perform small tasks, with the run ending here, or maybe a bar where he'd have to show me what he found, or maybe... Now, *that* orgasm was truly mind-blowing.

UNCHARTED TERRITORY

Evan Mora

She calls me at 10:38 in the morning, at work.

"I want your ass," she says.

That's all she says, all she has to say. It's not a question, and there's nothing for me to say except *yes*, so I do.

Hang up the phone. Make excuses. Meaningless words forgotten as soon as they're spoken. It's possible that someone will ask me about my so-called emergency tomorrow, but I don't care. This is what she does to me.

Sitting on the streetcar, head against the window, the slow west-to-east trundle drives me mad. I feel it already—the urgency, the need. The ache that starts in my cunt and radiates outward until my hands shake like a junkie who's past due for a fix. And I am. It's been more than a week. Long enough for the tenderness in my limbs to recede and my bruises to turn from purple to yellowish green, long enough for one ache to be replaced by another. That's part of it, I know. Part of the game that we play that is not a game at all. She makes me wait because I don't want to wait; because it's another way she can make me suffer.

My stomach flip-flops when we lurch to a stop across from her building. I clutch the upturned collar of my peacoat together at my throat in a vain effort to keep the cold January winds at bay, shivering as much with apprehension as from the temperature. It's an unsettling counterpoint to the arousal thrumming through me, this nervous thread of fear. Today will be different. She's been preparing me for this, has been from the start, but the knowing doesn't make it any easier. She doesn't want to spank me or sink her teeth into my ass—she wants her cock buried deep inside what, for me, is uncharted territory.

"Come in, boy," she says by way of greeting, turning to walk back toward the living room and leaving me to close the door and trail after her, the faint scent of her lavender perfume teasing my senses.

"Well?" she says, seating herself regally in a leather wing-back chair, crossing her legs above the knee, her black pencil skirt rising a tantalizing inch higher on her smooth, tanned thigh. She is an imposing woman, from the top of her salon-styled dark tresses down to the tips of her perfectly manicured toes—but it goes so much deeper than that. She has the kind of presence that inspires devotion and commands obedience. My devotion. My obedience. I swallow hard.

I undress under her impassive gaze, heart hammering in my chest. Tie, dress shirt, binder. These are the first to come off, folded neatly and placed in a pile on the floor. My nipples crinkle into hard points of arousal, and I blush to the roots of my short-cropped hair. Shoes, belt and trousers follow, and then all that remains are my snug boxer briefs. I draw a fortifying breath, then push them down and off in a single motion, laying them on the top of the pile.

The transition is the hardest part. Out there, in the world, my image is one of strength and confidence; but in here, with her, there is no room for imagery, only the most basic truth, stripped and exposed. The silence is deafening. I wish she would say something. Order me to kneel, tell me to come to her—anything. But she doesn't. Not yet. She just looks at me. I try hard not to fidget, not to cover my sex, not to let her see how she makes me tremble.

"Come here," she says finally, and I nearly stumble in my haste to get to her, relieved by the comforting familiarity of sitting at her feet. She strokes my hair idly and I rest my head against the side of her leg, kiss the skin there softly. She pulls my head back sharply.

"I didn't tell you to kiss me, boy," she says.

"I'm sorry, Mistress," I murmur. Her hand fisted into my hair feels amazing and my clit jumps at the little hurt. She shakes my head gently before letting go.

"Liar," she says, with a hint of affection. "We'll deal with that later Kai. In the meantime," she continues, "I want you to tell me how your assignment is progressing."

My assignment.

"It's progressing well, Mistress," I stammer, my cheeks reddening again.

Mistress Alessa told me when we met that she expected all of me to be available to her whenever she wanted. When she found out I'd never engaged in any kind of ass-play before, she'd smiled with delight, "Why, that's my very favorite thing!" she'd exclaimed. Penetration in general wasn't high on my list—I preferred to be the one *wearing* the cock—but in short order I found myself fucking her while her finger was pressed deep into my ass, and then, after a spanking that set my skin aflame and had me on the verge of orgasm, I was over her knee with her fingers pumping my ass, crying out and coming shamefully on her lap, tears streaming down my face. She'd sent me off that day with a fat anal plug and instructions to masturbate myself to orgasm every night with the plug deep in my ass.

"You've been practicing every day?" she presses.

"Yes, Mistress." I think even the tips of my ears are blushing.

"Excellent," she says. "Go upstairs and get ready for me."

Just like that? I pad quickly and silently across the hardwood floors and up the stairs to her master suite, my stomach a jumble of nerves even as my sex pulses insistently between my legs.

I stop short at the side of her bed. I know how she wants me: facedown, shoulders on the bed, ass raised; there are pillows piled neatly in the center of the bed with a towel draped over them to place under my hips, but that's not what has me frozen in place. There's a leather hood lying next to the pillows with only a thin slit for a mouth and what looks like a leather blindfold snapped over any eyeholes it might have.

I break out in a cold sweat. I can't do it. I can't pick up this hood and calmly put it on. I'm a wreck just thinking about offering up my ass to this woman, and she's got me so tied up in knots I'd do just about fucking anything for her. But this? It's too much.

"Is there a problem, boy?" Her voice is so close to my ear I jump, and then the words just spill out.

"Yes, Mistr—I mean *no,* Mistress—I'm sorry Mistress...I can't..." I'm wringing my hands, imploring her to understand, my whole body trembling.

She grabs me by the neck and pushes me down.

"Brace yourself," she says in a clipped voice, and I bend forward, forearms on the bed, ass pushed out toward her. I press my face into the mattress, squeezing my eyes shut against the stupid tears that spring up and then the first lash lands, a slash of heat and pain across the center of my ass that rocks me forward and has me biting my lip to keep from crying out.

She wields the leather strap expertly on my tender skin, covering my ass and my shoulders and then the more sensitive skin on the top of my thighs until I am crying out, tears falling in earnest, awash with misery and pain.

And then, just as suddenly, it stops. Chest heaving, I suck in deep open-mouthed breaths, knowing better than to move without her say-so, acutely aware of the heat emanating from my aching flesh. I hear her moving about behind me, but I'm unprepared when her fingers slip between my legs and into my cunt, and my breath catches in my throat with a gasp.

"Oh, you like that, don't you, boy?" she whispers against my ear, pumping in and out of me slowly, then drawing her slick fingers forward to tease my clit. I'm so hard it's almost painful and I whimper, hips rocking forward helplessly when she pulls my hood back and strokes my length between her thumb and forefinger. Her soft laughter caresses my neck as her fingers dance out of reach.

"So eager to come, and yet when I send you up here to get ready for me, I find you dithering about at the side of the bed." I moan against the coverlet as her fingernails scrape across my ass, and she gives me a hard pinch.

"I told you before, boy, that *all* of your holes belong to me, didn't I?" she says.

"Yes, Mistress," I gasp, as she pinches me again.

"Perhaps you need a reminder to help you remember that in future, hmm?" she purrs, delivering a sharp smack with her hand.

"Yes, Mistress!" I cry.

She kicks my feet wider apart, and then her pelvis is snugged up against my ass and the cool head of her cock slips into my cunt. I grunt into the mattress as she grabs my hips and pulls me back toward her, impaling me fully on her shaft. She fucks me deep and rough, hips slapping against my hot ass, then she leans forward, draping her torso across my back and slipping one hand around to squeeze my neck while she continues to fuck me, slowly cutting off my ability to breathe, the pressure in my head and my clit rising to critical levels.

"You belong to me, boy," she breathes into my ear. "Whenever and however I like." She sinks her teeth into the hollow between my shoulder and neck, biting down so deeply that stars explode behind my eyelids and I cry out and come so hard I think for a moment that I might pass out.

She eases her weight off of me, releasing her grip on my throat and withdrawing her cock while I half lie on the bed, panting like a dog, waiting for my vision to clear and wondering whether my legs will hold me if I try to stand up. I needn't worry though, because she orders me to kneel, and I sink gratefully to the floor at her feet.

"You really are incorrigible, aren't you?" She looks at me critically. "First you disobey me when I tell you to get ready for me, and then you come like a teenage boy without so much as asking me first." She tsks disapprovingly. "I'll have to add that to your list of transgressions, but we'll deal with that later. For now, I want to see if you can suck my cock without disgracing yourself any further."

"Yes, Mistress!" I say quickly, rushing on my knees to take up position before the purple cock glistening obscenely between her thighs. She picks up the leather strap in one hand and grasps the base of her cock with the other, slapping it wetly against my face while I chase it like an open-mouthed baby bird. She laughs at my eagerness, but takes pity on me and slides it into my mouth, farther than I'm expecting, and I gag, reaching out instinctively to grab her thighs. It's the wrong thing to do, and the strap falls smartly against my shoulder.

"Hands behind your back, boy," she says sharply. I quickly fold them behind me, moaning around her cock, the only apology I can offer with my mouth stuffed full like it is. With one hand she holds my head still so she can fuck my mouth, while the other wields the strap again, letting it fall rhythmically against my shoulders, left then right, in a way that feels almost like a caress. I moan again, with pleasure, losing myself in the myriad sensations flooding my senses.

"What a sweet little cocksucker you are, boy," she murmurs, and my clit pulses hard at the slight huskiness in her voice, a telltale sign of her pleasure. I'd suck her cock until my jaw ached if it pleased her, but all too soon she's pulling out, pulling me up by my hair and leading me back to the bed.

"You know what I love about you, boy?" she says, stroking my cheek gently. "I love how pain softens you, how it opens you up..."

She lays the strap down and picks up the hood, and I can't help but stiffen up again.

"Turn around," she says, and I turn away from her, heart hammering in my chest all over again, nervous sweat breaking out on my palms. She slips the hood over my head and laces it up snugly in the back. With the blindfold covering the eye sockets, I'm engulfed in blackness and I feel like I'm on the verge of hyperventilating when her soothing voice calls me back to her.

"Shh... Be calm, boy," she whispers next to my ear. "There's nothing to be frightened of," she says. Her nails are tracing sensual patterns across my back and chest, circling the hardened points of my nipples, dipping down to scrape along the sensitive skin of my inner thighs. I shiver uncontrollably, goose bumps breaking out on my skin.

"Feels good, doesn't it?" she says. I nod my agreement, my breathing slowing to something closer to normal. "I just want you to relax; really focus on the sensations in your body, okay?" I nod again.

She guides me onto the bed, positioning me on the pillows so that I'm where she wants me. I'm hyperaware of everything—the softness of the leather against my face; the coarser texture of the towel beneath my hips; the way my nipples just barely brush against the coverlet; the way the mattress dips when she moves into position between my thighs.

I moan softly when her fingertips feather lightly across my ass, and again when she spreads my cheeks apart, exposing me more completely than anyone has before. There's the pop of a bottle top opening, and I gasp as cold lube is drizzled onto my asshole. On the exhale it becomes a moan again as her finger gently circles my anus, dipping inside, spreading the lube thoroughly inside and out, sending frissons of pleasure through me. She works me well, fitting my ass with a plug and letting me have her cock in my cunt again, reaching around to work my clit, bringing me all the way to the peak again and releasing me with a soft command.

"Come for me now, boy," she says, and I'm coming in a perfect void of pleasure, spasming against her fingertips, her cock, the plug filling my ass.

And when I am emptied and relaxed, floating in the darkness inside my hood, she brushes the head of her cock against my ass, then slowly presses forward. It's bigger—so much bigger than the plug I've become accustomed to that my muscles instinctively tense again, despite her gentle foray.

"Relax, boy, just relax..." she whispers softly.

And I try, I really try, repeating the word over and over to myself, but as the head of her cock disappears into my ass

I think briefly, desperately, that I can't do this, that the pain is too intense. My hands clench into white-knuckled fists gripping the sheets and my safeword dances behind my eyelids and brushes against my tongue as pain knifes through my body. I try to breathe through it—I don't want her to be disappointed in me when this is so clearly what she wants...

But then a curious thing happens. As she slowly thrusts more deeply into my ass, the pain lessens, and exquisite sensations rise up to mingle with the pain. She's slowly but gradually increasing her pace, and sweat breaks out all over my body. My hips rise up to meet each thrust and I'm breathing open-mouthed moans into the bed in time to the rhythm of her fucking me. She's making breathy sounds of her own, and I can feel her pleasure rising and I am lost, completely engulfed in sensation, sinking into it, time and place disappearing until there is only her. Pleasing her. Giving myself over to her. She cries out suddenly, her body tensing above me as she reaches her peak, and I feel a pleasure, a *gratitude*, so intense that it transcends orgasm completely.

In the aftermath, I am still floating, only vaguely aware of her cleaning me, removing my hood and urging me to lie down beside her. Gradually, the sensation begins to ebb, and she kisses me deeply, exploring my mouth leisurely with her tongue, biting my lip almost playfully.

"What a delight you are, boy," she says.

"In fact," she continues, unbuckling her harness and laying her strap-on to the side, revealing the glossy dark triangle beneath; the swollen glistening folds, "I think you've earned yourself a reward."

And I rush to take my place, the swell of gratitude returning to fill all the space in my chest, as I determine to show her just what a good boy I can be.

SUFFER

Giselle Renarde

Every Sunday, Rex received his penance.

"I did it again, Sir." Naked, he kneeled in the center of Mei-Xing's dark sitting room, head hanging low. "Twice this week."

"Then you are suffering twice the burden," Mei-Xing reasoned. She was good that way, astute and compassionate.

Most people wouldn't understand how Rex could classify the woman who punished him as compassionate, but Rex wasn't like most people. He felt things very deeply. Shame, mostly, and guilt as well. Those were at the top of his list. Love was on there, too. Mei-Xing understood that. She understood that his affair was more than just a fling. He really did love Josephine, every bit as much as he loved his wife.

"I just couldn't keep away, Sir."

To some, it might seem strange that Rex called his domme "Sir," but that's the way she liked it. Far be it from him to question her motives; he trusted her too much for that.

"I understand," Mei-Xing replied, her voice soft now, a mourning dove's coo. "Your body is weak. Your mind is weak. You are a weak man, old soul."

"Yes, Sir. I know I am." He shook his drooping head, clenching his fists behind his back. "If I were stronger, I wouldn't have started up with Josephine. I'd have stuck by my wife. Eventually, I'd have gotten used to being sexless and lonely—that, or I'd have killed myself. The trouble is that I'm in love with Josephine. If I left her now I'd break her heart and break mine as well."

"But if you left your wife, same thing," Mei-Xing added, standing very close behind him. "You love her, too."

Rex turned, looked up, looked way up, and met Mei-Xing's gaze, though he really wasn't supposed to. Some would say Mei-Xing had a horse face, but Rex had never liked that term. And, yes, her face was rather long, but he appreciated it. The length made her seem stern. She wasn't a pretty girl like Josephine or a matronly woman like his wife, but maybe that's why Rex liked her so much. Mei-Xing was different. Her mouth rarely smiled, and it wasn't smiling now, but her eyes were. At least, they might be. Maybe. Mei-Xing was extremely hard to read.

"And if you left me?" she asked.

The question confounded Rex. "Why would I leave you? I *need* you. Without you, I'd just be a writhing mass of shame and guilt."

This time she smiled with her lips—a clear indication she was pleased. He hoped.

"Without you," Rex went on, "I'd probably have jumped off a bridge by now. I need my penance, Sir. I need to be punished."

"Good," she said. The word was like a gust of wind, explosive, and it made Rex's cock jump. He leaned farther forward and hoped she wouldn't notice his erection.

Rex didn't come to Mei-Xing for sex—he got enough of that from Josephine—but he did find her punishment arousing. The trouble was, his arousal here in Mei-Xing's living room made him leave feeling even more guilty than he'd felt when he came in. It certainly didn't help that she wore these striking leather getups to punish him. Today it was a skintight black bodysuit with one zipper down the front and another up the back. Rex wondered how she did up the back one on her own—she was single, as far as he knew.

Did Mei-Xing ever get lonely?

"How do you choose to be punished?" she asked.

Rex liked that she gave him the choice, even if he couldn't ask for the punishment he preferred. "The crop left marks, just like the whip. My wife would never notice, not in a million years, but Josephine asked about them."

"What did you say?"

"I had to make something up, Sir, and you know what a terrible liar I am."

"What did you say?" Mei-Xing repeated, her tone noticeably stonier the second time around.

It was so stupid that Rex didn't want to admit what he'd said, but how could he lie to the woman who doled out his punishment? "I said it was the guys at the gym, Sir. I said they were teasing me, cracking towels against my ass."

Mei-Xing laughed, but her grin was canine.

"Josephine didn't believe me," Rex went on. "So I had to show her. After we got out of the shower, I dried myself off, then wrung up my towel and whipped her ass with it. I've never heard her shriek like that, and her eyes went so wide I thought they were going to pop out of her head! Then I turned her around and told her to look at her ass in the mirror. She believed me after that. It was red as hell where I'd whipped her."

Mei-Xing sat slowly on the divan pushed up against the wall. It mustn't be easy to bend in that head-to-toe leather, but she managed. "Here," she instructed, patting her lap. "We won't leave any marks today."

"A spanking, Sir?" Rex crawled to her. "Sounds like just what I need."

Folding himself over her lap, he ensured that his cock and balls were hanging between her thighs, which she proceeded to close. The tightness of those leather legs around his straining erection and full, tender balls made him ache. He wanted to thrust between her thighs with every ounce of his being. He wanted to fuck that warm, supple leather until he blasted the carpet with cum.

But he wouldn't do any of that. He'd hold perfectly still while she brought down punishment on him. He wouldn't move a muscle.

"Tell me what it's for, Sir," he reminded her. "Tell me why I need to suffer."

"You suffer too much already. You bring your true punishment on yourself, with that little voice in your head that never gives you a moment's peace." This wasn't what Mei-Xing usually said before the pain began. "What I give you is not penance, it's pleasure."

Rex didn't get a chance to ask what she meant before her hand met his ass with a resounding crack. The first one never registered fully—its bark was worse than its bite. In fact, all he could feel was the blood whooshing toward his head, which was down on the carpet. He was dizzy already and suddenly confused. His heart seemed to be pounding in his balls.

The moment he tried to lift his head, Mei-Xing spanked him again. He felt it this time. There was a sting, an unmistakable bite that caught his ass when she struck it, and he hissed in response. Mei-Xing was strong. She could get through those lazy layers of flesh, the ones that sat in an office chair day after day, and make him faint with a smack of her palm.

Another smack. Was this one harder, or was his ass just getting more sensitive? He wanted to look back, see if it was pink yet. It didn't take long. After a few more spankings, his butt would be red as a cherry.

Another and another! Oh, god, it was starting to burn already, a slow tingle expanding outward from that point where her palm met his skin. Every spanking was a divine shock to his system. Each one gave him a jolt, propelled him forward, his forehead rubbing hard against the thankfully soft rug.

"Thank you, Sir!" Rex could feel himself squirming in Mei-Xing's lap, and before he could stop it she brought down another clap on his ass.

"Thank you for what?" Mei-Xing asked, tracing circles around his butt, dragging her ruthless fingernails across his flesh while he writhed beneath her.

His cock was straining between her thighs, and from his upside-down perspective, he could see a gossamer string of precum jetting from his cockhead all the way to the carpet. It was miraculous, like a spiderweb. The very sight made him forget all about Mei-Xing's simple question.

"Thank you for what?" she asked again, accompanying the question with a harsh smack. Mei-Xing never held anything back.

Rex cringed, grinding his teeth, tightening every muscle in the lower half of his body. When Mei-Xing spanked him with all his butt muscles clenched, it didn't hurt so much.

Stifling a tortured yelp, Rex said, "Thank you for punishing me, Sir."

Letting out a whiskey chuckle, Mei-Xing cast down the most

effective slap yet. It burned through him like fire, streaking across the topmost layer of flesh as it soared between his legs. His balls clenched so tight they felt like they'd shot back up into his body, and his cock jerked forward, whacking Mei-Xing's thigh, spreading that crystal-clear drizzle across her leather. Mei-Xing tightened up her thighs around his cock, trapping it in place. She said, "Nothing I do could be worse than the punishment you bring on yourself."

Rex puzzled over that statement while Mei-Xing traced her fingernails lightly down the backs of his thighs. It tickled when she got to his knee-pits, and his cock strained in light of that feathery sensation.

"What punishment, Sir?"

She spanked him, and that clap resounded through the room. Again. Again. *Smack, smack.* Her actions were measured. She never punished him in anger or ire; that wasn't her style. This was her job, her role in his life: to give him penance, to redeem him.

"You make..."

Smack!

"...yourself..."

Smack!

"...suffer."

Smack, smack!

His asscheeks burned, truly burned, like he'd been sitting on the stove. His flesh was on fire, and the pain was nothing short of torture. His brain buzzed as he listened to Mei-Xing's words over and over again, repeating them to himself like an echo in a cavern. His cock still ached for release between those leather thighs, but his body was the least of his concerns. Mei-Xing was right about his mental state, wasn't she? He made himself suffer, every day, with the guilt he held in his heart.

Suddenly, Mei-Xing snapped her thighs so tightly together that they compressed Rex's balls, making him shriek with pain. When he closed his eyes, he saw stars, constellations blasting across the dark backdrop of his eyelids, brilliant as diamonds.

"That hurts?" Mei-Xing asked flatly.

"Yes, Sir."

"More than this?" She slapped his blazing ass, and the stars burst into pieces, streaking across his mind like shrapnel.

"No, Sir." He always told Mei-Xing the truth. "The spanking hurts more."

She smacked his raging red flesh, and he jerked forward, writhing now, trying to escape. It hurt so damn much he couldn't stand it, but how could he hope to escape with his cock trapped between Mei-Xing's thighs?

"What hurts more?" she went on asking, setting her palm on his burning, prickling, hopping flesh. "A spanking on Sunday, or the anguish you suffer every day of the week?"

His head was heavy against the floor, blood pumping loudly in his ears. His heart was in overdrive, sending gushes one direction toward his head and the other direction toward his throbbing erection. His mind was hardly functioning at this point, just sensing pain and anticipating more.

Even so, he knew the answer to Mei-Xing's question. He told her, "Every day, Sir."

She traced her palm down his thigh, petting him gently while his cock ached for a release that wouldn't come. Mei-Xing only gave one type of release: relief from his sins, temporary escape, a chance to let someone else beat him up for a change. God knows he spent enough time beating himself up. He did it every day.

"Have you suffered enough?" Mei-Xing asked.

The question surprised Rex. That was her call, not his. "What do you think, Sir?"

Muscles tensed, ready for anything, he waited for some twitch in her body that would tell him whether she'd toss him to the floor or cast her palm down on his ass. She was still as stone, giving him no clue. His cock surged, ached, jerked forward as much as it could, but Mei-Xing didn't move.

Until she did.

Sliding her thighs open, she spread his legs enough to cast one small hand between them. Everything happened at once. Her flat hand landed hard against his tight balls, and lightning bolted through his veins. He yelped, trying to escape, but she had some inescapable magnetic hold on him. Rex stayed put, head on the floor, legs splayed, while Mei-Xing spanked his balls. It hurt beyond words, and the pain shot through him like an elixir. He wanted to be sick when she slapped him again. He wanted to roll on the floor and curl into the fetal position. Instead, he let Mei-Xing smack his balls again.

His muscles clenched, from his calves to his shoulders. When he opened his eyes, he was staring his cockhead in the face. It appeared closer than it was. It seemed near enough to suck. That wasn't the case, but something about the image of that giant erection fucking his throat put him over the edge.

Mei-Xing spanked his balls, just softly this time, and it was over. All over. His dick surged with cum, spewing the white stuff directly at his face, creaming his cheek mere seconds after he'd closed his eyes. Another shot blasted the ridge of his nose, creeping hotly down his forehead. After that, the surges of cum must have struck the carpet, and he'd certainly pay for the mess as soon as Mei-Xing noticed.

Somehow, he ended up fully on the floor, rolling from his back to his front because his ass burned so badly. He'd come so hard he couldn't move, couldn't even open his eyes as his cum turned cold against his face.

"I've never..." he stammered, not knowing how to complete that sentence. "I've just never..."

Mei-Xing took a warm cloth to his face and then to the carpet. She said, "You needed release, old soul."

He thought his pain was buried deep enough, but she always found it. She brought it to the surface, and today she gave him every kind of relief.

How did she know? How did she know what he needed before he did? How did she know things he'd probably never have figured out on his own?

With a compassionate smile, Mei-Xing read his mind and answered, "Old soul, I've suffered, too."

SUBDAR

Rachel Kramer Bussel

Some people like to think they have gaydar; Quinn *knew* she had subdar. She could tell within a minute of meeting a guy whether he was less interested in sitting across from her, staring passionately into her eyes, or perhaps taking her across his knee for a sadistic spanking, than in kneeling at her feet, head lowered, ready to bend over and grant her access to his beautiful bottom or to bend farther and kiss, lick and all-around worship her feet. She had a hunch about which men wanted to be blindfolded, bound, stripped bare in every sense of the word, handing over their autonomy to her to do with as she pleased. She could tell which were the types who wanted her to stop them in mid-sentence with a well-timed pinch of their arm; a warning hand resting on their cheek, threatening to slap it, in private or public; or fingers digging into the back of their neck, sending them halfway to ecstasy. It was a game she played when she was bored, whether sitting in traffic, at the real estate office among her coworkers or shopping in the mall—it wasn't hard to tell the subs among the men waiting with their wives' purses next to them in the department stores—or, like tonight, at a dinner party she was wishing she hadn't agreed to attend.

Subdar wasn't a skill she could teach other women, and even if she could, she wasn't interested in sharing her secrets. It was more of an innate talent, something honed over twenty years as a practicing dominant woman, from her first lover, Martin, in college, who'd begged to eat her pussy for hours, who she loved to tease by tying him up and using all manner of vibrators while he watched, helpless with desire, to the other men who'd longed to suck the cock she loved to wear. They wanted her to spank them hard and put collars around their beefy necks, and generally got off on giving in to her in every way. Something inside her, something more than just her pussy, lit up in the mere presence of such a man, even if he was already under orders from another woman. Seeing a man catering to a woman fed something in her soul, made her feel at home, whether it was an elegant woman in heels towering over her husband or simply one who knew how to twist her man to get her way.

Dominant women aren't always the bitch goddesses they seem in pop culture; true dommes know there are infinite ways to get what they want, and sometimes all it takes is a wicked smile or a hint of a whisper. Quinn considered herself a spy when out and about in mixed company, always searching for her peers, or a single man aching for nothing more than a woman to put him in his place. There were few things in life that gave Quinn the same kind of satisfaction as surveying a room and making eye contact with a man who fit her profile, who could feel the energy passing from her body to his. It made her wet every single time.

Tonight, though, she'd been thwarted so far in her attempts

at making such a connection. She'd even pretended to get lost and entered the kitchen, seeking perhaps a smoldering chef who could handle the heat behind the stove as well as in the bedroom, or a waiter who wanted to offer more than food service. Or a waitress; Quinn preferred male subs, but willing women were also delectable creatures to torture and torment. But alas, she'd found no one to play with so far, and she was restless. If this dinner party was going to be a dud, she might as well be home soaking in her bathtub, then relaxing with her favorite nonhuman sex toy, her plug-in vibrator. She worked extremely hard at the real estate firm, outselling her peers almost every week, using those feminine wiles she'd honed to sweet talk men into buying bigger and their women into picturing themselves as queens of their castles, and on the weekend Quinn sought to release all the sexual energy that built up when she wasn't able to use it properly.

She could smile and make conversation like the best of them, but she was bored and horny, and if there wasn't anyone here who could satisfy her in that way, she just wasn't interested in staying. Quinn had already scoped out the room and found nothing but vanilla guys and men who got off on *her* coveted role, dominating their wives or girlfriends or playthings du jour. Quinn had subbed a time or two, and could appreciate what women got out of it, but that was nothing for her next to the thrill of total control. And then, just like that, as she lifted her salad fork to her lips, something stirred inside her. She looked up and noticed a man with salt-and-pepper hair entering the room, a phone to his lips as he whispered urgently into it, while smiling at their host in apology. Quinn's nipples hardened instantly, and her pussy got wet when Andrea rearranged the seating so the mystery man could take his place next to her.

"Sorry I'm late, everyone," he said.

"No need to apologize, Roger," Andrea said in her sweet way.

"Actually, there is," Quinn leaned over and whispered directly in his ear, making sure her lips brushed his skin, before sliding her hand onto his knee to give it a squeeze. Both the whisper and the touch on his knee were brief, ephemeral almost, except she knew she'd made her point when he turned to her, his face growing red. He locked eyes with her as a waiter deftly placed a salad in front of him. Quinn raised one eyebrow, then deliberately turned away and struck up a conversation with the gentleman on her left side.

She knew her first volley had been well played and that Roger wasn't going to be listening to a thing Andrea said, or tasting the food on his plate. He'd be waiting for her, waiting to see what she'd do next, how she was going to command and control him. Quinn, herself, was calm for the first time all day. Having this man, albeit a stranger, sitting next to her, practically trembling in her presence, brought the opposite of shakiness. Roger's appearance gave her a surefire knowledge that her night was about to turn around, whether she bound and gagged him and simply enjoyed the pleasure of his cock inside her, or took him across her knee; or went harder, deeper, probing his mind and body in ways he likely wasn't expecting. It was the power that motivated Quinn, the power that Roger had already given her in their silent but extremely clear negotiation. The way his eyes kept darting toward her, the way he stilled when she put her hand on his knee, the way Roger passed her the salt when she requested it, then said nothing as she sprinkled it all over his plate—Quinn was a goner. Her subdar was like one of those carnival games where you swung a hammer or sprayed a water gun and the temperature rose to the top until a bell went off. Her bell was ringing, loudly, and she was pretty sure Roger's was too—and if it wasn't, she was going to make it ring.

Suddenly Quinn was wide-awake, glad she'd chosen to attend this dinner. She was an expert at multitasking, so she made conversation and didn't even mind that it was dull because what was happening between her and Roger was anything but. She managed to reach for him multiple times, grazing along his lower half—his foot when she dropped her napkin, his inner thigh when no one was looking, his calf with her toes when she shifted in her seat just a little—and smiled to herself when he dropped his own fork against his plate. He'd barely touched his food. "It's bad manners not to finish your meal, Roger," she said, in the same tone of voice one would use to scold a child. Her nipples hardened as she said it, and as she watched him rapidly pick up his fork and shove a large bite of steak into his mouth, she could already picture herself pressing her breast into his mouth, commanding him to take as much of it as possible then ease back and suck her nipples exactly the way she liked. She summoned the waiter, winking at him as he poured her more water, making sure he saw her hand once again claiming Roger's thigh. She knew he'd never tell; her subdar had found its second and, she was pretty sure, only other victim of the night.

Roger finished his food and looked at her for approval. She longed to lean over and kiss his forehead; in lieu of that she said, "That was wonderful," out loud, ostensibly to Andrea, but really to Roger. When she stood to go to the restroom, she raised her eyebrow at him to let him know he was to follow in a moment. She slipped into the bathroom and left the door ever so slightly ajar for him to slip inside later. She was grateful for the long, empty hallway separating this room from the dining room.

As soon as he was inside she pressed him backward against the door and locked it. She reached down and felt between his legs, grateful he was as hard as she'd hoped, both for his cock's usefulness later, and because she wasn't interested in ordering someone around who wasn't getting off on it; that wasn't fun at all. It was the thrill of the voluntary chase that turned Quinn on. "Get on your knees," she said, smiling as he immediately sank to the floor, his several-hundred-dollar suit now pressed against the sleek gray tiles. She slowly raised her skirt and lowered her stockings and black silk underwear, standing for just a moment so he could see her naked, then lowered herself onto the toilet. Her bladder was full, but she took her time peeing, as the sound and smell filled the room, making sure Roger was fully aware of her power. To his credit, Roger kept his head tilted down; he didn't ogle her or give any hint at his own arousal, but one glance at his crotch gave that away. She thought briefly of squatting over him, letting loose with a rush of her fluids straight onto his body, and couldn't resist the moan that left her lips. Quinn smiled as a corresponding shudder passed through Roger's body. Quinn ruled the room as surely as she had the dinner table.

She stood, fixing him with her eyes to make sure he stayed in place, as she washed her hands and added lipstick and gloss. Her pussy was throbbing at the proximity of this man who'd so willingly given up any shred of power he'd walked in with. She started to wipe her hands on the luxurious, deep-gray hand towel, then thought better of it and headed toward Roger.

He did look up at her then, as her heels click-clacked on the tile floor. She walked right up to him, resting her knee against his chest before reaching for his jacket and wiping her wet hands on the inside. "You don't mind, do you, Roger?" she asked, raising her hand enough to rest it against his neck.

"No," he said as she squeezed gently. "Ma'am," he added. She let her newly manicured nails stroke the tender skin of his neck, then gave him the lightest of slaps on his cheek. His eyelids drooped with desire.

"Now here's what's going to happen. I'm going to walk back out there, and in five minutes, you're going to follow me. You're going to make an excuse to leave once you return, and then you're going to go here," she said, whipping a pen out of her purse and scrawling an address on his inner arm. "Tell Maurice, the doorman, you're part of my special victims unit, and he will let you into my apartment. Take off your clothes and kneel just like this right in front of the door until I get there."

She didn't tack on a time; she'd get there when she got there, and she knew from the many other subs she'd entertained that the uncertainty was part of what got them off. Following her lead, and trying to figure out her next move, were part of what kept their mind and body in sync, like a kinky chess game, except she would always be the queen, the one in total control.

Quinn headed back out to join the others, smiling coolly as she took a creamy mouthful of her chocolate mousse. She stayed for the barest minimum of politeness then made a face that she hoped looked apologetic enough, before slithering toward the door.

"Give him a bit of a hard time when he tries to leave," Quinn whispered to Andrea with a wink as she walked through the door, her body abuzz as she headed out into the crisp night. Putting men through their paces always fired her up, made her come alive, let her know that kink was what she was designed to do. It was as if she could feel the nervous, excited energy radiating from his body straight into hers, charging her up like a battery while he trembled in anticipation.

Quinn forced herself to sip a very leisurely latte, fantasizing about the barista who looked barely out of college, making sure Roger had plenty of time to follow her instructions. She could've stayed at dinner, but there was no point; there wasn't anyone else there she wanted to talk to. When her drink was done and she'd undressed the barista so thoroughly with her eyes that the young woman had blushed, she headed toward home, walking faster than usual, her heels clicking a beautiful staccato in her ears. She hadn't told Roger that she actually had a separate apartment, next door to hers, one for guests or lovers, or, in this case, herself. She'd originally bought it as a financial investment, but it had turned out to be an investment in kinky play, and scenes she had never anticipated when she arrived. She too would be waiting, her heart pounding, for Roger to enter her door. She'd never tell him or any other sub, but waiting was a challenge for her as well. Quinn was an impatient domme, eager to get to the heart of the matter, but knowing that the longer she waited, the greater the reward would be for both of them.

Sometimes she thought the best part of being kinky was the anticipation, the savoring of what was to come; yet, as delightful and delicious as her fantasies were, a live, drooling naked man, eager to hear and obey her every order, his neediness practically vibrating through the air, always won out. She was full of energy, so much it could've powered a jog around the block, but instead she entered her spare apartment and cooled down by making sure she was prepared, rummaging in her bag for the nipple clamps she always kept stashed there, along with a mini vibrator, some lube and condoms. Just like with the lottery, you never knew when kink would find you. She hoped Roger was good at licking pussy; it was pretty much job requirement number one for a good sub, in her opinion.

When she was certain Roger was inside, having heard a nervous cough of his, she quietly exited the apartment. If the floors hadn't been carpeted, she'd have made sure her heels clicked loudly back and forth in the hallway, giving him a hint of what was coming. Quinn knew how to dominate a hallway, even the few steps next door, and had the perfect heels for it. She loved the idea of instilling the perfect combination of fear and excitement in Roger, but there was also something exciting about him not knowing when to expect her. Instead she turned the key quickly, eager to survey her new sub. Sometimes a scene didn't go as planned; the man fumbled in his nervousness or discovered he wasn't quite as needy in real life as in his fantasies. But in seconds, Quinn saw that Roger was perfect, as was his cock, which stood straight up. His hands were placed behind his back, like they belonged there, and Quinn couldn't help the grin that spread across her face. While she found images of women with their breasts thrust out in that position commonplace and clichéd, a naked, erect, kneeling man never failed to make her body ache.

When she detected the slightest hint of trembling in Roger's otherwise proud posture, Quinn knew she was going to come hard. She walked over and thanked him by shoving two fingers deep into his eager mouth, already picturing those same fingers sliding between his buttcheeks. "Get down on the floor and show me what that tongue is good for," she said, and Roger did so immediately, without question. Quinn did indeed come fast and hard, a shock even to her, but she went on holding his face there, needing more. He ate her for a half hour straight, with short breaks for breaths of air, before she let him up. Then she led him to her bedroom, where she tied him to the bedposts and made him watch her come a few more times using her favorite vibrator. Every once in a while, she granted him a teasing taste of the vibe along his balls. She'd instructed him not to make a sound, but he only lasted a few minutes before small whimpers escaped his lips, much like the precome escaping the tip of his cock.

"I could tell exactly what kind of man you were when I laid

eyes on you," she told him. "It's obvious, so there's really no trying to hide it." She pulled him close, his erection pressing against her hip as he laid his head in the crook of her neck. She would ask him later if he wanted something more permanent. For now, his quiet subservience was enough to tell her everything she needed to know. He wasn't going anywhere.

GOOD FOR THE GOOSE

Kathleen Bradean

He meant it as a joke, I'm sure. He *better* have meant it as a joke. Maybe I should ask Mike. The poor dear can't answer right now, so I'll save the question for later.

I remember those *True Confessions* magazines at the supermarket checkout when I was really young, and the way the headlines always fascinated me. Just the idea of confessions was exotic. I was brought up Southern Baptist, so we didn't have confession or hoity-toity Latin or any of that fancy stuff. If confession at a Catholic church were anything like those tabloid headlines, I imagined being a priest was one heck of a cool job. I mean, people would come in and just pour out all their lurid sins. Like the best gossip, ever. Right? Who cares if the pies Mrs. Smith brings to the bake sale are store-bought? She might be a swinger, or better yet, a part-time prostitute.

And I, my delicious friend, am going to tell you something that's worth a few—what do you call 'em?—Hail Marys. We're paying you for a full hour, so sit there nice and quiet as a priest and just pretend to be interested, because I'm going to make a confession for Mike.

So, Mike here: one night he's watching television, as usual, and ignoring me—as usual. And then he leans over and puts his hand on the back of my head and gazes into my eyes and I think, oh boy, this is kind of romantic for him. And then he shoves my face down to his groin! But that's not the part that got me riled. No. He unzipped his pants and shoved his pecker into my mouth. He'd been working in the yard and was a bit ripe, so to speak. Still, I wasn't upset. I was a little turned on, to tell the truth. Getting a little wet down there, you know? So I figured what the heck and licked him a bit. He kept that hand on the back of my head and picked up the remote and flipped channels. As you can imagine, that was when I got good and steamed. You'd think a man would have a bit of common sense. There I was, with my mouth around his precious bits—a mouth full of teeth, need I remind you—and he had the nerve to pay more attention to a rerun of an old TV show than to me.

Well, I hit the roof. Sat right up and grabbed the fucking remote from his hand and told him that if he wanted me to suck his cock, he better turn off the damn TV and devote his attention to my loving ministrations—or else.

Mike had the good sense to lower his gaze and mumble an apology. *Didn't you dear? Just nod.*

Anyway, I'm a good sport, and as I said, I was turned on, so I smacked his knee and told him to get on into the bedroom so I could give him a decent blow job without distractions. He ran! That was kind of hot.

I took my sweet time walking down the hallway. By the time I got to the bedroom, he'd pulled off his pants but not his black socks. Ugh. His legs hung over the side of the bed and he leaned back on his elbows. There's a full-length mirror on the wall so he could watch me suck his cock. He really got off on that.

Didn't you, dear? Are you drooling again? Wipe your mouth and chest off with your towel. I don't care if it's stiff. Maybe next time you'll remember to throw it in the laundry.

I swear, teaching him responsibility for his cum rag has been quite a trial for me. As soon as he shoots his wad, he forgets. And if he thinks I'm going to touch that nasty, crusty thing...

So I knelt on the floor between his legs, and I started off by working my tongue over his balls, when this long old pubic hair got in my mouth.

Does that happen to you a lot in your line of work? I'm sure you have to be discreet about it with clients, but I don't, so I said, "Good lord, Mike! That's enough to make a girl swear off oral. Why don't you shave your balls? I trim my pubes for you. You could at least return the favor." And do you know what he said? He said, "If you want them shaved, why don't you do it yourself?" Well. Did you ever?

Then I was back to being steamed again because of his whole attitude. So I stood up and said, "All right. Maybe I will." And I marched off to the bathroom and grabbed a razor and a towel and some shaving gel.

His eyes were wide as saucers when I got back. But his cock didn't look scared at all. No, sir. Not one bit. His cheeks were rosy and he couldn't quite look me in the eye.

"What do you want me to do?" he asked, all quiet and polite. I liked that. Liked it a lot. So I told him to spread his legs and tucked the towel under his butt so we wouldn't stain the linens. Then I put a little dollop of the gel on my hands and spread it around. But I couldn't reach everything so I told him to draw his knees up to give me better access.

Then I knelt down again and took the razor to him. Gently.

I was still a little ruffled, but you know, I love him and didn't want to hurt him or anything. Truth be told, I was scared I'd nick him, so I kept running to the bathroom to rinse off the razor. And I took forever because I was being so careful. About half way through, he told me that he couldn't hold up his legs any longer.

Was it your idea or mine, dear? Tying you up? I don't remember.

Doesn't matter. Next thing you know, I have one end of the tiebacks from the living room drapes looped around each of his ankles and the other ends around the bedposts. We've since bought some nice ankle cuffs and straps, but for the first time, the tiebacks worked out really well. Mike's legs were spread wide for me. Made it so much easier for me to shave him. And that whole time I was shaving him, once he was tied up and I didn't have to worry about him moving, I was just getting wetter and wetter.

Are you gay for pay or really gay? Because I won't bore you with details of how tingly it got me if that's not something you're interested in. But if I was one of those girls who could come just from rubbing her thighs together, I would have taken care of business in about two seconds. As it was, my hands were busy, Besides, I figured if I was doing all this work just to get to the point where I could blow him, then there was no way in hell I'd let him roll over and fall asleep without getting me off.

Mike really liked the warm water rinse when I cleaned the shaving gel off him. But then he said his balls were cold. Poor thing. And he started complaining about his feet going numb. Said all the blood had rushed out of them from being up so long. Uh-huh. I knew exactly where all his blood had gone. His cock was casting shadows like a sundial.

I bent down and ran my tongue over his balls. I tell you,

now that I've had the pleasure of tasting shaved, I won't lick a hairy ball ever again. He quieted down for a while but started complaining again. He started squirming and trying to get free.

I smacked his butt and told him to settle down. He got a funny look on his face. Then he started squirming some more. Sort of like he is now.

For goodness sake, Mike, hold on. We'll get to you.

You'll have to excuse him. I swear, he just does it for attention. He's fine. He's used to being tied up so maybe having his hands free is too much for him. I'll take care of that right now.

Mike, you know the signal if your hands go numb, right? Good boy.

There. Tied up like a birthday gift. See that hard-on? He loves his rope.

Anyway... Mike was putting up such a fuss that I told him I was going to give him something to really holler about. If I thought his eyes were big before, they got *huge* as he watched me suck my finger. I let him see in the mirror as I pressed it to his tight little hole. Didn't even go inside. Not like I do now. He can take three fingers, easy. Did I say easy? He likes my knuckles slamming against him as I ram my fingers in and out of him, hard. But that night all I did was press my finger to it and he quit yelling and twitched a few times and shot his wad all over his belly and some even went flying over his head and landed on my pillow, I found out later.

So I untied him and rubbed the circulation back into his feet and boy howdy, did I get some servicing that night! That man was grateful, that's for sure. I was so turned on that it didn't take long, and when I came, my eyes about rolled back in my head. For a minute, I thought my heart would pound out of my chest.

We didn't talk about it for a while, then he got all shy one night and asked if I could shave him again, and maybe spank him a bit more. A bit more!

You sure do like a good hard swat on the butt, don't you, sweetie?

I can tell when he wants it because he starts acting all surly and doesn't take out the garbage for a few days. He likes to be over my lap. We even bought him a special hairbrush. He loves that thing. Keeps it in a velvet bag in his sock drawer.

We've been doing this for a little over a year now. Trust me, he wouldn't dare watch a rerun over my head anymore. And we've been quite happy. I tell you, just thinking about tying him up gets me so wet now that I had to figure out how to bind him so he could still service me. Aren't my knots pretty? I took a class.

Life is really good, but one thing has been kind of hovering at the back of my head this whole time, and I figured it was time to work it out. Carrying around old resentments is just bad for a marriage. Don't you think?

So I told Mike it was time for him to learn what it's like to have your head shoved down into a man's crotch. I want him to know how difficult it is to give a quality blow job. Don't worry. He agreed to it. I can be quite persuasive.

He picked you out, you know. It was the cock shot in your profile. Don't get angry, but it's because you're normal sized. He didn't want anyone too hung. And I thought you were just so cute in that picture you took in your bathroom mirror. I love the ink on your pecs.

Let me just take the ball gag off Mike. Then I'll go sit over there and watch. Be sure to shove his face down on your cock and force him to stay down there. Teach him how to do it right. Don't allow him to get away with giving bad head, because I sure as heck never gave him a lousy blow job. And I hope you didn't shave your balls, like we discussed. And you haven't bathed for a couple of days, right? He needs to get the full effect of what he was asking me to do.

There's an extra fifty in it for you if you trick him into swallowing.

ALL EYES
ON HIM

Aimee Nichols

1

I know enough about university lecture theaters not to roman-
ticize them, not to think of them as hallowed halls of learning
so much as holding pens for bored, spoiled undergraduates, but
even so I'm surprised by this one. It's huge for an arts subject
lecture venue, which suggests that this subject attracts a large
enrollment; that this lecturer has important things to say. It's
barely one third full, however. I know it's the shockingly early
hour of 10:00 a.m. on a Tuesday, but I still would have thought
that the students could rouse themselves out of bed for the man
who will be talking, the one I'm here to see. And the lack of
other bodies makes it harder for me to decide where to seat
myself. I don't want to be too much of a distraction. First year
poli-sci is serious business.

I decide on halfway back, toward the right-hand side.
He arrives just as I'm sorting out the notebook and pen I've
brought. Amongst the laptops and iPads, my paper is downright

anachronistic, but it will do. It's a prop.

He radiates power, control; dominating his space, commanding attention from every mind in the room. It makes me wet.

2

His message stood out to me. So many of the men who contact me seem to fail at basic reading comprehension. They top from the bottom from the first sentence; they fail to realize that I, too, am human, and seeking to meet my own desires, not just theirs. Worse still are the dominant men who are sure that they can be the ones to change my mind, make me learn that what I really want is to be dominated, not to dominate. The ones who feel they can break me.

In contrast, he was polite, measured, and respectful to the point of obsequiousness. The fact that his profile showed him to be deeply into or curious about some of my favorite things and his photos showed him to be attractive in an unconventional way didn't hurt either.

He might not stand out to you, if you saw him on the street going about his day. But he stands out to me, when we are together, and he stands out here in this auditorium.

3

I know our first coffee meeting involved some good conversation, but the memory of what was actually said remains ungraspable, copied over and erased by all that has come since. I know he was charming, polite, eager without presumptuousness, honest and genuine in the small details he gave of his everyday life.

We met on neutral ground like the sensible grownups we are, but it didn't take long before I knew I wanted to take him home and fuck him.

After we finished our coffees, I asked him, point-blank, if he wanted to come back to my house. His hands shook a little as he said yes. He'd driven to our meeting place and as he drove us back to my place I took note of the way he took directions easily, open to listening.

I tied him to the bed with silk, as I am a sensualist at heart. As the last knot closed against his skin, a nearly visible change took place; I felt him relax into the edge of subspace. I stroked his face and murmured sweet nothings; he nuzzled my hand like a calf. I trailed my fingers down his chest, stroking gently, until I came to his nipples. I gave a tiny, playful pinch, and watched his cock jerk in response.

"Do you like that?"

"Yes."

I pinched harder. "Yes, what?"

"Yes, Ma'am."

His cock jolted to full attention as I gave a sharp twist, and he let out a little moan.

I climbed up to his face and straddled him, holding myself up so that my pussy sat above his face. Looking down, past my tits, I saw him staring at it with hunger. I lowered myself onto his face and locked my thighs around his head, feeling his ears press into the soft flesh of my inner thighs. He licked me, nuzzling his nose and cheeks against my cunt, and I sent a silent sinner's prayer of thanks that he knew what he was doing; his tongue explored me expertly, flicking in and out of me as I rode his face, feeling my orgasm mounting. My muscles began to pulse, signaling something more powerful than my average orgasm. As I rocked against his face, I watched his hands clench into fists and strain against his restraints, his unconscious urge to grab me betraying him.

I paused, and whispered, "I see what you're doing there,

naughty boy. Do you want me to stop? Because I will. I can take my orgasms from any filthy boy I like."

He moaned, and his fists dropped back against the pillows. I resumed riding him as he lapped me, and soon my muscles gave one last clench.

With a gush, I came, spraying my juices over his face. I felt him gasp, and moved off him, lest I choke him with my arousal.

I looked down at his face, which was dreamy, cunt-struck.

"You're a gusher," he murmured, like one might wonderingly remark on the presence of a heretofore unknown species.

"Yes," I said, wiping my come off his face and pushing my fingers into his mouth. He sucked at them as I moved them in and out, miming the thrusting of a cock. He made a little noise, half whimper, half moan, and I smirked to myself. *I'm going to have fun with this one.*

4

He slips anonymously through other contexts. Here, and with me, he shines.

Sometimes when we are out together, I notice fleeting approving looks from other people, usually men. To a conventional eye, we make a fine couple. Enough of an age difference to look deliberate but not enough to look creepy to those who'd take offense. Even dressed casually, he clothes himself like someone used to power and fine things, like someone used to being looked at, but also looked to for approval. His personal style is understated, but evokes quality and assurance. I, admittedly, dress like a uni student. This is enough to fool the untrained eye, and looks like the kind of power differential that even completely straight people approve of, even if they do so unconsciously. This is the story we are used to. Women, especially attractive young women, are meant to be attracted to power. Men who make no effort to please anyone but themselves bemoan their lack of ability to get the women they feel they deserve: young women who are supposed to be attracted to their obvious power and virility. We're supposed to accept status and money in exchange for being dominated.

Some of us know that's not the only narrative.

I figured out I was dominant pretty early on, when I used to like to catch the boys, playing kiss chase in the schoolyard. Freed from having to be the ones always in pursuit, they would flee and squeal and flap as I would run them down, tackling them into the dirt, fighting with them until I felt that precise moment when their brains told their bodies to stop the struggle. Then I would look down at them, smile and climb off. I rarely kissed them. That wasn't what I was after.

I took an inordinate interest in being the cop in cops and robbers, and felt a smug sense of achievement when my victims were unable to get out of the knots I tied around their hands and feet. If I was feeling particularly unkind, I'd find something to gag them with, and watch as a range of possible emotions colored their cheeks first pink, then red.

At that age, it wasn't exciting, just…obvious. It was what I did. Other people existed for a range of reasons, but sometimes the reason was so I could hunt them down and tie them up.

It wasn't until hormones were added to the mix that tying boys up and occasionally making them cry became something far more interesting and complex than my childhood games could ever have hinted at.

And, of course, it's men like him that benefit. While most of the world looks at us and sees a story about a dashing older man seducing a younger woman, people in the know see that there are other stories at play; other ways for our narrative to get from beginning to end via all the interesting stops in between.

He's at the podium, leaning against it with elbows locked, thrusting his weight against it as he gives these first-years the Machiavelli 101 lecture that he must have delivered at least a dozen times by now.

I like to think that Machiavelli, with his intricate knowledge of power play and sardonic wit, would have been a kinkster himself. Or at least he would have appreciated what it is I do.

5

I take him to my favorite club, and all the way there, I can sense his fear. What if he is recognized? What if something happens to out him? What if, what if, what if?

Underneath the fear, lurking in the basement of the Escher-house of his emotions, is excitement. What if he is recognized? What if something happens to out him? What if, what if, what if?

I let him socialize as normal for a while; I haven't collared him tonight, and he comes across as harmless enough that even the shy newbies find themselves drawn into conversation with him.

I wait until I see that Xin has arrived. Xin and I dated briefly, but it didn't work out; we're both tops, and both volatile personalities. Topping helps me find equilibrium, brings a dynamic to a relationship that allows me to relax into things. I like to know where I stand with the person I'm fucking or playing with, and I like them to know where I stand, which, sexually speaking, is over them, and usually holding something used to inflict pain. Xin and I fucked like we wanted to destroy each other. That can be hot for a while, but it gets a little tiring. Neither of us was a switch in any way. The way we've learned to use our dynamic, our energy, is out at clubs, a tag team of pain-bringing and psychological fuckery.

I leave him talking to another sub about some TV series I haven't seen, a sweet woman who, unfortunately for me, shows no signs of bisexuality whatsoever. Walking over to Xin, I watch him turn to watch me, one eyebrow rising as he takes in my step. Xin knows me well enough to know what my mood is by my walk. I feel my lips curve into a smirk as his eyes meet mine.

"You've got a new toy, haven't you?"

"Not so much new, at least to me, but yes, I've got a good toy to play with tonight. New to here. New to most of the things we could probably think of for him to do."

"Excellent. What do you have in mind?"

"Nothing that will make him wish he'd never been born. Maybe enough to make him, very briefly, wish he hadn't met me. He doesn't know much about pain at the moment. I thought maybe that's where you could come in."

"Well, it is what I do."

"It's what you do best."

"I know it."

A short time later, the flogger dances across my toy's back, a ballet of pain and lust. I watch the set of his shoulders as I work; I can almost feel the gasping breaths he takes to work his way through the pain, working through his urge to beg me to stop, wanting to make me proud. We amass an audience, and I find myself tamping down my urge to perform; the theater of the public scene has always drawn me in, but I try not to let it draw me in too heavily.

He cannot help but arch his backside out to me; his desire to be spanked has transcended consciousness. If I stopped the scene right now and told him to stop presenting his ass unless he wanted a finger up it, he'd probably deny he was doing it, and from his perspective, he'd be telling the truth.

Keeping the flogger going, I beckon Xin over.

"How do you feel about administering a spanking?"

"I feel pretty good about it. You think he can take one? You know how I give them."

"I think he can take it."

I slow the flogger down to let him know there's going to be a change, and stop it completely.

"Xin is going to take over from me for a bit. Are you going to be a good boy for him?"

He nods, and I take his chin in my hand and turn his face to me. I stare into the embodiment of happy subspace; his eyes are dreamy, and a faint, goofy smile plays across his face. I kiss his forehead, and he murmurs a thank-you.

Xin nods as I move away, and steps in. He whispers something in my toy's ear and I see him give a faint nod. Xin begins to stroke his buttocks then warms them up with quick, light spanks.

The sound of the first hard slap ricochets between the bodies gathered watching the scene; I see a few people who are familiar with Xin's work wince, and I allow myself a smirk of pride.

They don't have much time to recover, however, as Xin's work happens thick and fast. My man is a trooper and presents himself for the onslaught. His ass pinkens, then reddens, and I can see him bracing himself. Xin works harder and faster than I could, an entirely different type of top. Soon I can hear the recipient of Xin's labors gasping, his breath coming out in little convulsions as his brain tries to deal with the onslaught of pain signals and their accompanying, contrary pleasure. The physical manifestations of this psychological drama are some of my favorite things to watch. The sub's dilemma: *one more slap, and I will call the safeword and stop this. One more. One more. One more.* And one more, until the idea of the safeword becomes unconscionable, as the pain and lust and joy merge into an all-encompassing world of sensation.

I can see that Xin is enjoying himself immensely. His pain lust supersedes any gender-based sexual orientation; his erection strains against his pants. I alternate my gaze between Xin's crotch and his work, and feel myself getting slick.

His ass is red, and the grunts coming forth are growing louder and less for show. I give Xin time to finish up; he notes my nod and slows things down, moves back to tenderly stroking his victim's asscheeks. He leans in and speaks again; I see a nod. And then Xin is bringing him over to me, laying him across my lap to inspect his handiwork, and stepping away for us to reconnect as domme and sub.

"You're mine," I breathe, as he sobs and convulses across my lap, both sets of cheeks red; shaken and reborn. I muse on the aftertaste of those words in my mouth. I have never said them to anyone before. I am surprised to find I mean them.

6

I wait. I don't want to make my presence known yet, not enough to intrude on his space.

As the students begin to pack up and ramble slowly out of the theater, I watch him watch them, taking in the extent of his audience with a mild, benevolent gaze. If he feels any contempt toward them, any boredom at running through the same lecture and being asked the same questions again and again, he does not show it. He is every inch the twinkle-eyed, leather-patched professor.

The theater is still a good quarter full when his gaze finally finds mine. I stare him down and watch him freeze, eyes widening, posture stiffening slightly, like a hunted creature who's just sensed a predator. Holding his gaze, I throw my legs over the seat in front of me so that he can see that I've worn my boots, the ones that he likes, the ones that bite so hard into his skin. I watch him take in the challenge in my eyes. A few remaining students stare at me as they walk past on their way out, most with no real curiosity, some probably wondering who the random goth is and why I don't have black hair or pale makeup. Out of the corner of my eye, I see one girl twig to what is happening, staring first at me, then him, then turning to her friend to whisper. No doubt she thinks that I'm seeking power or a better grade. She is wrong.

I stand up, taller than usual in the boots. The cotton ruffles of my skirt swish against the bare skin of my thighs. I lift my skirt and show him, show everyone, that there is nothing underneath it. He is not the only one who has frozen now; all eyes are on the girl holding her skirt up around her waist, the girl who has no knickers. I can hear little intakes of breath; feel scorn and amazement and disbelief. And I turn and leave the theater.

I count under my breath as I walk down the corridor, then smirk as I hear his footsteps behind me.

BLAME
SPARTACUS

Laura Antoniou

I see them all the time now, blockbuster movies filled with preternaturally handsome twentysomethings masquerading as teenagers in some futuristic dystopia, or manly hunks in skimpy loincloths and sculpted armor hacking away in CGI-rendered stadiums on giant screens or via my deluxe cable-TV package. It's so very chic today, to enjoy tales of epic personal battles for the pleasure of a bloodthirsty audience. This is quite an improvement from the time when the very phrase "gladiator movie" was a not-so-sly comedic reference to homoerotic diversions.

Erotic, yes. And while I appreciate the fact that my gay male friends also enjoy the scenery—and the scenario—I am not a member of that team. I'm straight, if someone as kinky as I am can be called that. And I'm definitely a woman. I can show you proof.

But only once the battle has been fought and won.

* * *

I blame *Spartacus*. Specifically, I blame Kirk Douglas. Not that there's anything wrong with the current crop of *Sparticanni*, they are all quite handsome and well worth the subscription to premium channels. But I can remember the exact instant I became alive and aware of my fascination with men who would enter combat for my pleasure.

It was on a Saturday night when I was around fourteen or fifteen, on the threshold between going out with groups of friends and being invited on solo dates. That night, though, I had no planned adventures, and wouldn't have wanted to go if I did. I was home aching with my period, feeling uncomfortable and bloated; tired, cranky and unloved. Flipping channels on television, I saw images stream by, second by second, not even really registering anything on my way to find MTV or some other usual distraction. Then, my brain picked up on something and I clicked back and back again...and there he was. A broad-shouldered man with an enormously cleft chin, barely dressed, scuffling with another man in the dust.

I lingered, watched. Even then, there was a spark. My period aside, I was a healthy girl with a solid interest in the male form. One of my girlfriends had shared some pictures she'd found online and saved, in those days before we all had smart phones, on a disk. The two of us eyed the men's bodies with curiosity and immature longing. Men were so much more interesting than boys our own age, we agreed. And for me, unspoken, a little additional twist. Men *who would do what I liked* would be the most interesting of all. What I actually liked was still academic. It was the nature of obedience that turned me on, even back then.

That night, watching the men fight on my television screen, I realized something else.

I liked to watch men grappling with each other.

I kept the television on that channel and wound up watching all of *Spartacus*, the 1960 film directed by Stanley Kubrick. Oh, it was filled with stars of enormous magnitude! Laurence Olivier! Peter Ustinov! Charles Laughton! Even skinny little Tony Curtis. And while the older, less shapely men draped themselves in bedsheets, the fit and muscular ones stripped down to leg-baring loincloths and leather straps across their upper arms and chests. But even better—they stripped down and picked up weapons and fought each other for the amusement of the better-clothed, aristocratic spectators who wagered on the matches.

I remember holding the remote in my hand, frozen in place, watching the screen flicker. The training regimen; the small dark cells where the gladiators lived, the casual way a woman was thrust into a cell like a hotel housekeeper delivering extra pillows. The different styles of combat—with a short sword and shield, or curved sword and greaves, or spear and net!

Oh. Oh, to be a spectator there, leaning elegantly over my seat to pluck crisp, cold grapes from a tray; to sip blood-red wine while I watched men pant and growl and circle each other like animals. To *own* one of those men and place a coin down while laughing, betting with my friends who would fall first. To see my man, my property win, and take my winnings and take my gladiator home, and...and...

I must have been fourteen. I don't remember actually imagining what would happen beyond kissing him. But in my mind, he would be a much better kisser than Terrance Galbraithe, my on-again, off-again, almost boyfriend.

The gladiatorial fights end early in the movie and then it becomes a vast adventure tale that ends badly for all the slaves. But it didn't matter; I was hooked. I no longer wanted just any good-looking man to populate my nascent fantasies; I wanted a gladiator. I wanted a man who would fight for me, because I told him to. Or because he wanted to please me and gain my favor.

I became a fan of boxing, wrestling and martial arts in general. Fencing became so much more interesting when I fantasized knights and musketeers dueling for the opportunity to woo me. As my body and tastes and experiences became more mature, my fantasies remained solidly in that realm. And the first time a boyfriend of mine actually did vow to kick the ass of any other boy who looked at me, I must admit it was thrilling for the moment.

And then I decided he was a posturing ass. Shortly after that, I realized I would never actually *experience* this fantasy. I truly didn't want a real man who would go out and hurt someone else and risk harm to himself, arrest, shame and the reputation of a macho jerk. I scolded myself for even harboring such fantasies and tried to write them off as the longings of a girl-child unaware of real-life values. They were as foolish, I decided, as lusting for vampires, or pirates.

Cody is slender and carries himself with the precise grace of a tightrope walker; his unstylishly long hair is fine and colored like honey fresh from the comb, run through with strands of corn silk. He wears it clubbed for Revolutionary War reenactments and most of his friends and coworkers think that's why he has grown it out.

But I love trailing my fingers through it when he is on his knees in front of me or leaning against my leg while I read or watch a movie. I also enjoy watching him run across dusty fields in period uniforms, a Hessian mercenary or a Redcoat. I never lost my taste for costume dramas, and he always has a movie or a series or a book for me and can regale me with folklore and amusing tales like a modern Scheherazade.

And he looks so appealing in the wrestling singlet I ordered for him online, nothing but cobalt-blue Lycra cupping his cock and balls and his sweet, pale ass; with straps framing his body, curling over his shoulders and crossing his back. His stomach and chest are bared for me, shorn even of the light, pale hairs that barely dusted them. Low, light boots are on his feet and a soft suede collar, the same color as the singlet and lined with a layer of brushed cotton, is tight around his neck. It fastens with Velcro, because it's just for decoration. He might earn the chain if he rises victorious.

Cody came in answer to my ad on one of the alternative sex websites. Sorting through dozens of poorly written notes, hundreds of messages from men who hadn't bothered to read my actual ad and thousands of pictures of penises yielded me exactly one man who had lasted beyond my layers of getting-to-know-you filtering. Cody not only wrote complete sentences in English, he addressed me respectfully and included in his first note to me not a picture of his gonads taken while standing at his bathroom mirror, but the shot of him holding a trophy and wearing a *gi*. He had a bruise under one eye and was grinning madly.

He read my ad.

I discovered the world of alternative sex and BDSM where everyone else has—online. Idly browsing one day, I had put "sexy gladiators" into a search engine and expected the usual array of photos from old Italian sword and sandal movies. Instead, I found a gay porn website of men wrestling and then getting it on. The clips I saw had me as frozen in place as my teenage self years ago. But this time, I had a credit card. This time, I could stop the action, and start it again and see the whole thing. Every glistening inch of manly flesh displayed for me in the privacy of my home, as they rolled and grabbed and grunted and growled...and then...

And then they fucked.

Usually the winner got his cock sucked or got to use the loser doggie style, but sometimes that seemed to shift into mutually pleasurable acts. I knew my preference at once. The winner had to get something, yes, but the loser had to *suffer*.

And by the way, I still needed to be in charge. How to manage this took a while to figure out. It took my discovering that I wanted more than an acquiescent lover in my bed. I wanted—I desperately wanted—two men, competing to please me: one to win, and the other to suffer.

For my pleasure. And while there is nothing aesthetically displeasing about watching two men engage in enthusiastic sex with each other, I would prefer that at least one be paying attention to me. While the other suffered.

See the theme?

Alvaro was a furry man, but not with the wiry, bristly, coarse fur I personally find unattractive. His was jet black and straight along his forearms and down his calves, dusted across his chest and then down the center of his hard stomach like a cross, to expand in a bush around his cock and over his balls. I had him clip that area short, but not shave it. The fur there and across his round asscheeks was just as pleasing to me as the silky hair on Cody's head. Alvaro, older than Cody and shorter, was also more stocky and muscular, and the hair on his head was receding. This he also kept short, along with the line of hair along his jaw, a sexy strap of a beard and a mustache to match.

Alvaro did not take me to war-games or regale me with tales of Revolutionary derring-do. But he made me *caldeirada*, brimming with chunks of lobster and whole tiger shrimp, he found rich red wines to entice my palate and rubbed my feet and temples and back with consummate skill, humming lullabies and love songs under his breath.

I met Alvaro at a fetish party; I was in a long black leather gown that laced up the front and sides. He was dressed as a *luchador* from Mexico, only his trunks were black latex, as was the silver-streaked face mask. I asked him if he wrestled in real life as well, and he grinned behind the mask, his teeth showing the gleaming uniformity of crowns. "I wrestle and box!" he told me making a muscle with one firm bicep. "Do you like to watch?"

"Yes," I replied, running a finger down the center of his chest. "Yes, I do."

Tonight I have made Alvaro wear the scarlet singlet, boots and collar. My boys had arrived nice and early. Cody cleaned a bit, moved heavy furniture, sorted out my recyclables and updated my calendar on the computer and my phone. Alvaro roasted potatoes and eggplant and medallions of veal while his wine breathed and flan set. Cody drew my bath and left me soaking to a mix he'd programmed onto my iPod; when I got out, Alvaro met me with a warm towel and soothing almond oil to rub into my skin before I dressed for dinner.

My boys have learned to share as well as compete. I brought them along slowly to understand that my desires cannot be filled by one man; I had to have at least two. Four would be better. But *if* they kept me diverted, then perhaps I could make do with only two.

The heady port served to me after dinner was not nearly as intoxicating as the entertainment to follow. My men, facing each other, dressed as I pleased, eying each other warily, ready for my word to begin. Furniture had been moved to create their battleground, leaving me to recline, Roman style, their single spectator.

"Freestyle," I finally said. It might have been Greco-Roman, collegiate or grappling. Alvaro had started judo classes; Cody had taken up boxing. It was my plan to be able to watch them in a mixed martial arts matchup. It was my dream to offer them up as a team against some other gladiatorial-minded collector of fighting men. One day, I will find someone else, I'm sure. In the meantime—they will wrestle for me.

Freed from a formal first position, they each feinted forward immediately, then danced lightly back. Neither one was fool enough to fall for the feint; I found it delightful. I sipped my sweet port and nodded as I watched them circle each other, shoulders hunched, eyes darting, hands flexing.

Cody made the first real move, charging forward in a spear, trying for a double leg pin. But it was far too early and Alvaro turned aside easily and grabbed for Cody's shoulder, propelling him farther and faster and straight down to the floor. Cody hit with a slight stumble and in an instant Alvaro was on top of him looking for a pin.

But Cody was wiry-strong and flexible; he twisted and squirmed and got one elbow braced and bucked back; I could see the tension all through his arms as he put all his strength into pushing Alvaro off of his back. He kicked out one leg and caught Alvaro between his, and in an instant, he rolled and knocked Alvaro off. Pulling his limbs in like a shocked tortoise, he rolled backward and leapt up in a gymnast's move that made me applaud with glee.

Alvaro shot an arm out to try and grab Cody's ankle, but Cody leapt out of the way and then dived down to throw his body against Alvaro's. Alvaro was trying to rise, and Cody's lighter form slammed against his bowed back, but Alvaro didn't even pause. Cody scrambled to try and grab an ankle, an elbow, but his moves were in vain. Alvaro simply rose to his knees with Cody still draped around him; he reached out and back and found Cody's slender arm and one leg and twisted and grunted and brought the younger man up and then threw him down onto his back!

Oh, bravo, I thought, my eyes wide and my thighs wet. *Yes, pin him now, press him down, flatten him!* Did I cry out loud? Sometimes I did. Sometimes, it all stayed in my head, along with the roars of the stadium behind me.

They squirmed and struggled together. Alvaro's buttocks shook and clenched as he tried to pin the ever-moving sinuous body beneath him. Cody planted his boots and arched his back and then brought one knee up sharply, slamming Alvaro in the hip.

"*Caralho!*" Alvaro exclaimed with a tooth-baring grimace. In flinching, he lost his hold on Cody's legs and the lithe younger man twisted like an eel and sprang back, panting.

"Yeah, fuck you too," Cody snarled.

Alvaro darted forward to grab one of Cody's legs, but he was off balance and breathing hard. Cody hip-checked him and tried a toss, but Alvaro's weight and strength didn't allow for an easy lift. Cody gasped as his lift failed and Alvaro laughed and shoved his back against Cody's chest, crowding him toward the center of the room. Cody took the shove and was already slightly off balance when Alvaro elbowed his way inside his defenses and slammed him down hard onto his back, Alvaro splayed over him.

Alvaro didn't stay there, though; he hammered that elbow back one more time, forcing the breath from Cody's mouth, and then turned and grabbed him and lifted one leg while pressing his shoulder down.

"One," I said idly, running a finger down the front of my blouse. My nipples were hard enough to ache. "Two…"

Cody tried kicking, he tried squirming and he slapped his free arm against the floor in frustration. Baring his teeth again, he growled and fought, but Alvaro stubbornly set his muscles and weight against him and would not be moved.

"Done!" I pronounced.

Alvaro immediately let him go and Cody cursed, his fists tight, face flushed with the shame of being beaten, the frustration of loss. Now my own hunger grew like a wild thing; caged for the civilized courses, let free in the darkness of my fantasies. Were those tears, or beads of sweat on Cody's pink face? Either would please me, but both made my body ache with need.

"Again," I said. Waiting would make my play sweeter. "Greco-Roman. Begin."

Quickly, they shuffled, took the first neutral position and moved in on each other looking for an arm drag. Now there could be no leg grabs, nothing below the waist. This left their clenched asses flexing under the iridescent stretching material of the singlet, their unfettered cocks and balls bundled loosely and exposed as clearly to me as though they were out and dangling. I had seen versions of the singlet with a hole for a man's package to poke through, and had occasionally considered buying some. But there was a visual pleasure in watching their flesh so barely contained by that sheer fabric, noticing the appearance of a hard-on or the absence of one. Alvaro, I noticed, has a few drops of moisture making a darker spot on his gladiatorial uniform.

That was because he had won. I watched them slip in and out of grips on their upper arms and shoulders, like some strange, angry dance, and selected a thin chocolate from the plate next to me. In the split second of my attention being drawn away, Cody darted in, grabbed Alvaro's left wrist and pulled, hard, and turned in a neat, economical circle. Alvaro seemed to be able to follow through toward recovery, but then he stumbled, and Cody immediately pushed that same arm and leapt forward, adding extra force and momentum to the move. Alvaro went down so quickly all I saw was a flash of his boots, and then Cody was on top of him, spreading his arms and keeping his legs away from any pinning position.

Such a good boy!

"Bravo!" I finally said aloud. "Cody, take the bottom position."

His grin of victory quickly vanished; Alvaro was better on the bottom, having more strength. But Cody needed the practice. He got onto his hands and knees, shaking his head and blinking; Alvaro quickly got into the reverse lock position, tucked alongside Cody's body, facing his ass. Taking a deep breath, he leaned over the younger man and locked his hands around Cody's waist. I took a slow, deep breath. My personal porno channel was right here.

"Begin."

Cody immediately seemed to go limp as he tried to pull his whole body flat to the carpeted floor. This might have lost an opponent the ability to do a simple and clean lift, but Alvaro was ready. With every muscle on his beautiful back he strained and pulled and plucked Cody up off the floor and into the air. Cody tried not to engage his legs in fighting back—if he kicked Alvaro, he'd lose right there—and in his panicked distraction could do nothing but grimace as Alvaro rotated his powerful shoulders and slammed him back onto the floor. It was a beautiful move: perfectly executed, skilled and savage.

Did I have it in me to wait for one more pin? My nipples said no. The way the wine had gone to my head and the chocolate melting on my fingers—had I forgotten to eat it?—told me no.

And I didn't have to wait. They were my gladiators.

I extended my chocolate-smeared fingers and beckoned to Alvaro. "Look what you've done," I said. "Had me so mesmerized I wasted my chocolate. Clean that." He eagerly took my fingers into his mouth and suckled and licked, panting around them as he tried to control his breathing. I withdrew them, and wiped them idly on the strap of his singlet. "Bring me three things," I said, leaning back on one elbow. "For Cody."

Cody had already brought himself to his knees, his face a mask of disappointment and shame. I breathed in the scent of his body and shook my head. "You must learn to win from the bottom," I said, pleased that he'd lost. Last time, he'd taken Alvaro down in two out of three matches before my lust declared him the winner and interrupted the match. He'd chosen a butt plug, a cock cage and a whip. Silly boy. Alvaro had liked all three.

And he had his revenge at last. For he returned with a slightly larger toy meant for insertion—one of those vibrators that shimmied and wiggled. I had found it too distracting to use for my own pleasure and had thrown it into my toy box without remembering it for some time now. Also in his hand was a pair of clamps with weights and a blindfold.

Oh, clever Alvaro. Now Cody wouldn't even be able to watch.

I beckoned to Cody and handed him the garishly colored vibrator. "I suggest you put a condom on this and lubricate it before you present your ass to me." He nodded and whispered, "Yes, Ma'am," before he took it and scampered off.

"And what shall we do with you tonight?" I said aloud, rising to allow Alvaro to undress me. "What has tonight's champion earned?"

"A kiss?" he teased, confident and proud. His cock jutted out like a horn, stretching the thin Lycra so much I could see the wrinkles made by his foreskin. I ran a finger neatly along each strap of the singlet and they fell down his arms and the garment bunched around the bottom of his ass. He drew my blouse off gently and unzipped my skirt.

Cody sucked in a breath as he came back into the room on his hands and knees. The controller box for the vibrator was tucked behind one of the straps of his singlet. So, he was being a clever boy as well!

Right then, I could have fucked them both. But rules were rules, especially when they were my rules. Cody lost. And now, he would suffer.

So he only saw my nakedness for a few seconds before I strapped the blindfold on. Then I put him on his knees with a pillow up between his legs to help keep that vibrator where it was so snugly fitted. I put a clamp on each nipple, and then clipped a weight, letting them bounce lightly in my fingers before releasing them. Then, my own touch, I used the thin cord I kept around just for occasions such as these and put a slipknot around the head of his cock. Disgraced or not, it was semihard, full of blood and stiffening at my slightest touch. Pulling it free of the singlet, I pressed the pale, curved column against his stomach and placed the end of my little cock leash in his teeth.

"Don't lose that," I whispered to him, as I found the controller box for the vibrator. I switched it on and heard the tiny little engine inside start to buzz. Cody jerked as it moved inside him and moaned around the cord in his teeth.

"Next time, you will fight harder," I said, not sure whether it was a command, a threat or an observation. Then I turned back to Alvaro.

"So, gladiator, have you earned the right to pleasure me?" I asked. I stood over him like the conqueror I was—owner of male flesh and bone, director of my own games. He looked up at me from his knees, his eyes bright and cock rampant.

"Keep that nice and hard," I cautioned him, as I slipped back onto my couch, one knee up, one leg down. I spread myself wide for him, a reward and a command and a threat and a promise. "Kiss me now, champion. Kiss me until I am ready to use that weapon you've got there and maybe I'll allow you a victory orgasm yourself tonight."

He crawled forward, even though he could have risen; he bowed his head to me one more time before his lips and tongue approached my pussy. He kept his hands away, one no doubt on that rampant cock, but touched me only to give pleasure, as I had taught him. I threw my head back and turned to see poor Cody, shivering and straining, his cock harder now, his hips moving and shaking the weights on his nipples, a circle of sensation and discomfort and shame.

I looked back and forth between the two, fortunate and tormented, rewarded and punished and both mine, all mine. My impatience rose again and I laughed in the shuddering aftershocks of my first orgasm. Reaching for a condom, I tossed it onto the floor next to the couch, then grabbed Alvaro's hair and kept his mouth pressed against me. "Again," I purred, in between gasps. "Again, one more time, maybe two and then my champion, maybe I'll use that cock…"

But there was no maybe about it. My men. My gladiators. My pleasure. I was the ultimate winner of every match, the way I always dreamed it might be.

Now, if I could only find out where one learned to fight with a trident and a net…

THE DINNER PARTY

Anne Grip

'm ready to leave."

I fetched Ma'am's coat and moved toward her but stopped short as I saw her under the hall light. She was dressed for a night out in a bold red-and-black floral party dress, but I had noticed the flowing fabric silhouetting a blunt object just to the left of her sex. Beads of sweat formed on my upper lip, and I swallowed hard. She smiled sweetly in my direction, her eyes glittering as she caught my reaction.

"Now."

I approached again, trying to look anyplace but where I had seen that whisper of a bulge pushing against her dress. As I held it up, she slid into her coat without a look back. Side by side we resembled any butch/femme couple you might see on the streets of Brooklyn. I wore a paisley bow tie, as they were having a fashion moment. Ma'am liked to have a stylish accessory at her side, or half a step behind in my case.

My shirt was one size looser on the collar than I usually

wear as it had to button around Ma'am's leather collar and the
metal lock that kept it in place, the key on a white gold chain
around her neck. It could stay there for all I cared. Nights in the
collar when she came to town were an altered state of being for
me, a reality I happily entered and never wanted to leave.

Wrapped in her long black coat, the only part of her outfit
still visible was her black, high-gloss shoes. Three shiny buckles
crept past her ankle to her lower calf, and the gaps between
each one showed a glimpse of fishnet stocking. Kneeling before
her I had pulled those stockings on and straightened the rear
seam before tightening each strap and fixing the buckles one by
one, enacting our dressing ritual, which began my service to her
before each date.

I was hers. Our signed contract had yielded my body and
will to her exclusive use. We were on month two of six. I lived
in dread of time passing and of me not measuring up to her
exacting standards. Any opportunity to serve her meant a chance
to show her that I was worth being signed away for longer than
a trial period and kept as a cherished possession or pet, to be
used however she desired.

I opened the door to the town car that had pulled up front,
helped her in and shut it. One night, our date had ended right
there. The car had pulled away and a text on my phone gave
me instructions to stay in the apartment until she returned later
that evening. I assumed the position on the bed as instructed
and waited. I had plenty of time to contemplate my devotion to
her, and by the time my phone buzzed with my next instruction
I was delirious with want.

Tonight she gestured me forward, and I got in the black
sedan from the other side. I looked to see if I should kneel on
the floor or stay seated beside her. "That's fine," she indicated
and I stayed put on the seat, thankful to not have to deal with

the unsavory floor of the car service. She smiled with a look of vague serenity that meant puzzle pieces around her were falling into place.

"Look over there." I turned to my left and the view out the window was replaced by the darkness of a blindfold. "That's better, now isn't it?"

"Yes, Ma'am." Better, sure, but more nerve-wracking. I wasn't a control freak by a long shot, but this was like that moment in the roller coaster where the big bars clanged down over your chest and you were strapped in for the duration of the ride. I felt her hand slide up my thigh and give it a firm squeeze, fingers digging into the inside. Then she let go and tousled my hair.

"Such a patient boy you are, well behaved too. You're going to make me proud tonight, aren't you?"

"Yes, Ma'am." Not knowing what was in store for me, I felt confident that I was well dressed, well behaved and obedient enough to handle anything that came up. Ignorance, as they say, is a boy's bliss. The car jostled through Saturday-night traffic somewhere in the city, presumably still in the askew grid of Brooklyn since I hadn't felt us climbing any bridges.

The ubiquitous pine-tree air freshener overpowered the enclosed space, but I could feel Ma'am's heat beside me, even though we were no longer touching as she steered us toward our unknown destination. Without my sight I felt myself breathing deeply, searching to bring her inside of me. It kept me from wondering where we were going, as I sought her scent as my talisman.

"On the left side," she instructed the driver. The door was opened for me and I followed the sound of her voice in a reverse parody of my earlier chivalry. "Lower your head." Too late. A branch brushed against my cheek. "Step down." I did. A gate clanged behind us. I continued my tentative walk, trusting in Ma'am, but convinced of my own clumsiness. I moved as though my ankles were hobbled.

I felt the air change and heard another door close behind me. The space was warm, and I smelled the aroma of freshly roasted vegetables.

"My coat." I turned toward Ma'am's voice and removed her coat as easily as if I had use of my eyes. I held it out once done, and it was taken by someone who wasn't Ma'am. "Yours as well." Again the jacket was lifted by the silent person. Ma'am maneuvered me through the space, this time with her hands on my shoulders, heading farther from the cooking dinner. Now I could smell the rich amber of scented candles.

"Handsome as they are, you don't need those street clothes any longer." I removed my boots and pants, untied my bow tie and unbuttoned my shirt.

"Boots back on, boy." I awkwardly stepped each foot back in and laced them up. Finished, I stood at attention wearing a snug-fitting pair of white A/X trunks, a white A-shirt and of course my collar, locked in the back. I bowed my head and waited.

Nails began to etch down my bare left arm. Hot breath sighed against my face. Scratching began on my right side as well. Ma'am was not immediately near me. So there were at least three.

"Such a treat you brought for us tonight. And just in time for hors d'oeuvres," the voice at my right rasped. Ma'am had friends in the city. None of them were people to whom you would entrust anything small or helpless. At the moment I felt both.

"Poor thing must be starving, coming out for dinner so late." This was the voice at my left. She was badly feigning an interest in my well-being and the dissonance set off a shiver.

"Oh, and cold—how terrible! We don't want to neglect this charming toy you brought along." Her voice trailed off, "Poor little...starving...boy..." Fingers dipped into my mouth that I hadn't realized was open.

"Hungry boy." Right Side growled again, her mouth close to the side of my face. I smelled the aphrodisiac chemicals of lipstick.

"Yes, Mistress," I choked out, hoping this was the correct address.

"I can tell." She gave a soft squeeze down below and scraped her nails under my tightly pressed package. I whimpered as her hand pushed my cock into my pulsing clit. "Well, don't want to keep a hungry boy waiting," she snarled and two hands shoved hard against my chest. I fell backward in a panic and landed on a bed immediately behind me.

Three voices cackled in unison and I recovered from my fright, biting my lip to hide a smirk as I lay flat on my back among them.

"I'm first." Left Side moved over me and I felt her straddle me with plush thighs strapping me down. "Let's warm up the jaw." A slap across my face rocked me from right to left. That was for her pleasure, but my cunt gushed from the impact. She shoved her fingers inside my mouth again, and I eagerly sucked.

"So hungry." Fingers removed, a slap came from the opposite side. I let my neck sway with the blow, stinging this time, wet from my saliva. Again she fed me fingers, this time probing deeper. Again I opened for her, feeling the tickle in the back of my throat and the submission that suppressed any gag reflex. I had just begun to suck again when she pulled them back a bit.

"So eager. Let's see how warmed up he is." She climbed higher on my body until she straddled my upper chest. Something very large began to push into my mouth. It stretched the corners tight, and I felt fear. *Ma'am won't let me get hurt,* I told myself. But Ma'am couldn't see the size of what was being shoved into my mouth with the domme perched atop me, and the panic swelled up again.

"Open sesame, you little cocksucker," she commanded from above. I forced breath in through my nose and worked on relaxing my throat. That was the only trick I knew. I hoped it would help with my jaw as well. The very fat cockhead, if that's what the monstrosity was, popped in. It couldn't fit much past that, as it seemed to get even wider. She rocked slowly on top of me, fused to my mouth, dirty talking about how hot my hole was and how I wanted to take it all inside. No way was any more of that going to fit in me. Yet her words had their effect. I wanted to take it all. I stayed open, eager to make Ma'am proud that she had a good, obedient boy who could take whatever was served up.

Someone seized my right wrist and put my hand on another cock. The same happened with my left. Both pricks were lubed up and I began to jerk them off, gripping firmly, pumping up toward the head. The one in my right was rigid, and I pumped faster. The left side, was this Ma'am? I didn't recognize the shape or the feel of this prick, softer on the outside with a pronounced curve upward. I bore down, grinding it against her clit the way I knew she liked, but also squeezed up and felt it respond as I did, almost like it was growing in my hand. I worked all my parts in unison, sucking and jerking. Still blindfolded, I pictured how Ma'am's lips parted when she was aroused. Whichever hand held her, I put all my effort into serving her pleasure, hungry for her come.

My own spit drained from both corners of my mouth, the flow seeping into the crevices of my ears. Tears pooled behind the blindfold from the strain of the rod fucking my mouth. I could feel myself drift away to a happy place where my only role in life was to serve femme cock, where I would be held down and forced to submit to their hard-edged drive until they each had their fill.

"You were right. Nothing is too big for this boy whore," spoke the voice from the domme astride me. The frenzy paused. My mouth was unplugged, and I panted to bring in some of the oxygen I had foregone. Her thighs, now slick with sweat, dismounted and I felt lost without my rider.

Before I had time to wonder what was next, I was pulled off the bed, more or less upright, and frog-marched a few steps forward. Impatient hands pulled down my underwear and I was thrust onto a body below me. I realized I was astride the femme with the massive cock as the hardness stopped me from below.

"You know what to do." Ma'am's command left me frozen. I was afraid of being impaled on that huge member, but nowhere near as frightened as I was of ever disappointing Ma'am. I parted my asscheeks with both hands to spread my cunt as a willing offering and lowered myself. I groaned as gravity forced me open wider but gave a full-throated yell as strong hands held my hips and brought me firmly down around it. I sobbed from the violation but groaned again as she lifted me up and I felt the fullness slide away. "Ohhhhh, fuuuuuck," came gasping out of me instead of an exhale.

"Is it always so chatty?" Rigid silicone smacked me across the face. I felt weak from the huge plug that held up my weight and the proximity of more hard femme cock. "Suck it, boy whore, you can sing for us later." I opened up and dove forward to fill my throat with the slick smoothness of the femme's cock I had jerked off. She grabbed the back of my neck and fucked it in with rough thrusts.

I felt a familiar grip pulling the hair on the top of my head, the only place it was long enough for her to get a handle. "Mmmm, good boy."

I don't know what that feeling is when I hear her voice, when I feel her power. It's like the piece of me that has been missing my whole life has finally been inserted and I am made whole. She knows that I will do anything to serve her, however she wants it. She was happy. I heard it in her voice, felt it while captive in her grasp as the scene of her making was unfolding before her. The devotion she had kindled and fanned burned through me. My mouth crammed full, I could no longer speak so, "Yes, Ma'am," came out of my pores for her. It came bursting out of my heart along with the juice from my cunt and the drool leaking from my mouth.

"Take my come, boyslut. You've earned it." Ma'am's hot jism flowed across the side of my face and down my chest. My body shuddered in an abrupt orgasm from being filled, used, owned.

I hadn't asked permission to come. I would pay for that later. The blindfold was pulled off my eyes and all I saw was Ma'am—flushed, delighted, carnivorous. She bared her teeth in what would never be mistaken for a smile. Our dinner party had just begun.

FEAR NOT

Andrea Dale

Public speaking is the number one thing people fear, according to various statistics and surveys. Ranking higher than death, snakes and spiders...stage fright tops them all.

So when my darling husband, who suffers from glossophobia, received a well-deserved promotion that would require him to do the occasional presentation in front of various numbers of people, something had to be done.

Thankfully, he didn't have to give any presentations right away, which gave me time to prepare.

The first thing I did was have him write me a proposal of his own, detailing all of his deepest, darkest sexual fantasies. Not necessarily the things he wanted to do, but the things that turned him on the most. (Sometimes fantasy is enough, and we could discuss where the lines were if I chose to explore further.)

When he finished, I didn't even read it.

"Here's the thing," I told him that night when he'd done a most excellent job of licking me to multiple orgasms, after which

I'd ridden him to several more of my own, finally taking pity on him and allowing him to come. "You have to be motivated. And you have to get it over with. The first time is always the hardest. But I'm afraid *hard* isn't what you're going to be for a while."

He was still tied to the bed, which made it easy for me to slip the stainless-steel chastity cage over his flaccid penis. His blue eyes widened as he realized what I was doing.

"Mistress…"

I've had him wear the cage before, for short periods of time. Normally we didn't go for long-term orgasm denial—I allow him to come after I'm satisfied, like tonight. Or we play with multiple orgasms, over and over until he can't stand it anymore.

"You're wondering how long you have to wear this," I said, uncuffing him from the bed and helping him sit up. "It's simple. I'm going to set up an open mic night at the dungeon. I won't set the date until you tell me you're ready. That night, along with the other performances, you'll read the essay you wrote for me."

I patted his captured cock. "Until then, you don't get to come. *That's* your motivation."

I'd let our friends know about the open mic night plan, so they had time to prepare, too, and it wouldn't take as long to coordinate once my husband named the date.

I was pleased with the arrangements I'd made. Our local dungeon was once a multilevel nightclub, and we often used the low stage (formerly where bands played) for demonstrations. I'd procured a mic and sound system, and I made sure whatever other props people wanted were available.

Sometimes we opt for leather, but not this night. This gathering was more casual, and he'd be sweating enough as it was. He wore jeans and a T-shirt to the dungeon, and once we were there, he took off the shirt. I buckled his collar around his neck—again, it's not something we require, but sometimes it reinforces the agreements we've made in our relationship.

And besides, he looked so adorable, the blue leather highlighting his eyes and setting off his tanned skin and the dusting of dark hair on his chest.

The final thing I did was order him to pull down his jeans. He wasn't wearing underwear, at my previous request. Now, I pulled the key from my pocket and freed him from the chastity cage.

His cock sprang free and, just from the brush of my fingertips, bobbed toward erection. Not all the way, though, and I watched as he carefully tucked it in his jeans before buttoning them back up as instructed.

He hadn't been allowed to touch himself since I'd locked him in it, and I'd removed the cage only when he showered—under my strict supervision.

"Soon," I promised. "Just think, this will all be over soon."

He'd opted to go last, though, which was both a blessing and a curse. It gave him more time before he had to face his fear—but he also had to sit and squirm, listening and watching everyone else.

There were readings of erotic poetry and stories; there were bawdy songs, and a dance by a woman wearing nothing but toe shoes and a tutu.

Another woman recited something from memory while her mistress spanked her, the look of concentration and lust on her face priceless, and I wished *I'd* thought of it. Perhaps it could be further training for my husband.

For many, it was an excuse to parade their submissive around in a cute outfit (or little-to-none, or elaborate rope bondage, et cetera) onstage. A few doms even got into the spirit of it and performed, including one who read a touching paean to his sub.

Two performances before he was supposed to go on, my husband and I went to the little backstage alcove. He looked down at his papers, over at the stage, and promptly ran to the bathroom.

When he returned, his eyes were glassy and his temples glistened with perspiration.

I took his face in my hands, forcing him to meet my gaze. "You're going to be brilliant, darling," I said, and I meant every word of it. "Remember, these are all your friends out there—they support you as much as I do, and want you to succeed." I patted him on the cheek and lowered my voice. "Besides, think of the reward you're going to get afterward."

I glanced down. Despite his nerves, his cock pulsed.

We'd discussed it ahead of time, and he'd told me he'd be more comfortable if I didn't sit in the audience. If it made him feel better with me in the wings, so be it.

And then he began to read. There wasn't much that surprised me, although I mentally noted a few details here and there. We were normally very open with each other; communication in this type of relationship is crucial.

The difference was that he hadn't expected to share this with anyone else...much less present it before an audience.

He wanted more punishment, more pain—crops and canes and whips, oh my. He thought trying sensory deprivation might be interesting. He wanted to play with butt plugs and anal sex more often. He wanted a Prince Albert, something we'd been discussing.

He was intrigued by public humiliation...and the way he glanced out at the audience then, for the first time since he'd started, made me realize this might be intriguing indeed. He went into some detail about that, such as being made to wear loose pants and be teased to visible erection, or being left outside while naked, or to have an obvious leash emerging from his pants.

His penis bulged harder in his jeans as he continued, and I heard his voice get stronger as he gained confidence. The people in front of him were his friends. Many leaned forward, listening intently. A few smiled encouragingly when he paused, and he stood up straighter.

I hoped he knew how proud I was of him.

He read the final words and then, to my surprise, convulsively crumpled the pages in his fist. A split second later, I realized why.

I'd made it abundantly clear that he wouldn't be allowed to come until he made his presentation. Clearly, that rule had worked its way deep into his subconscious.

Because without any touch from me or from him—without any external stimulation at all—he exploded into orgasm.

He screwed his eyes shut, his free hand gripping the mic stand so hard I thought it might snap. The look of release on his face was beautiful to behold. At first a low moan escaped him, but then all he could do was gasp in time with the spurts.

His hips thrust into empty air as his jeans stained dark with his semen.

It was the most erotic thing I had ever witnessed. I felt such an upsurge of pride and love and—yes—lust, that my whole body trembled.

His eyes opened, unfocused, and he swayed. Then, as one, the audience of our friends came to their feet, applauding and cheering. My husband finally came back to earth. His eyes widened, but he managed a bow before he literally ran offstage into my waiting arms. He would've knelt at my feet if I hadn't held him up, tight against me.

Part of me wanted to drag him over to the nearest sofa and have him bury his face between my legs. But as horny as I was, that could wait—for a few minutes, at least.

"I think," I murmured, "that we could call this a success."

At the same time, however, it occurred to me that I might have to rethink his training.

We needed to make sure he didn't get a steely erection—much less come, spontaneously and helplessly—every time he had to give a presentation at work.

LAYOVER

Lisabet Sarai

Y ou look good down there."

That's how it started. An accident, a bit of clumsiness on my part. I'd been bringing a couple of Cokes up to the cockpit. A stray breeze from a vent whisked the straws onto the floor. I was crouching, scrambling to pick them up with my right hand while gripping the tray with my left, when the door opened.

Captain Marsden's barely five three while I top six feet, but in that situation she towered over me. I froze, immobilized by embarrassment and sudden, inexplicable excitement. Sweat broke out on my forehead, and inside my regulation trousers my cock grew to distinctly uncomfortable proportions. I gazed up at her plain, even features; the reddish-brown hair wound into a knot and tucked under her cap; the familiar blue uniform—as though I'd never seen her before.

Her thin lips curled into a tight, knowing smile. Was the bulge in my crotch obvious? I struggled to rise. The cans of soda tumbled off the tray and rolled backward down the aisle.

The captain laughed, a clear, bright sound that sent shivers up my spine.

"Not exactly the level of professionalism we expect from our Shambala Air crew members."

I wondered whether I should go retrieve the errant cans. Trapped by her gaze, I simply couldn't. "No, Captain. I'm sorry. The straws..."

"I don't like excuses, Andrew. You'll learn soon enough to take responsibility for your errors." She gave me a frank onceover, a good deal less circumspect than the stewardesses who mooned over my blond hair and athlete's build. My pants grew unbearably tight. "I do think your intentions are good, however. You want to be of service."

"That's my job, Ma'am." I felt ridiculous, stranded there on one knee, crumpled straws in one hand, empty tray in the other. Something kept me nailed to the cabin floor. I didn't dare move without her permission.

"But I think it's part of your nature, too, to serve. Perhaps that's why you sought out this occupation." Actually, I'd applied to be an air steward because I loved traveling and figured I'd get a lot of pussy. I wasn't about to disagree with her, though.

"Hand me the sodas. I've got to get back to the controls." Her gaze held me fast. I groped behind me for cans. The chill metal burned my palms as I passed them up to her.

"Thank you. I have something for you, also." She pulled a black fabric bag from her uniform pocket, similar in size and shape to the toiletries kits we distributed in first class. "If you're serious about serving—put this on, and leave it on until we land. I'll give you further instructions then."

She disappeared back into the cockpit. The metal door clicked shut. It was easily thirty seconds before I was together enough to stand. I headed for the toilet, thinking I'd give myself some relief before returning to work. What I found inside the bag made that impossible.

I'd never seen a cock cage before, but the purpose of the leather and rubber device was pretty obvious. The largest strap buckled under my balls. The smaller loops encased my shaft in progressively tighter circles. A longitudinal leather strip ran up from the base, along the top of my rod, branching near the bulb into two strips intended to be fastened around my waist. This belt-like component pulled my raging erection tight against my belly. I worried the fluid leaking from my slit would make dark spots on my uniform, but what could I do? Perhaps Captain Marsden deliberately wanted to add embarrassment to my uncomfortable arousal.

Why did I follow her instructions? To be honest, I never considered refusing. Emma Marsden turned out to be right about me.

The remainder of the fourteen-hour flight was a kind of lustful hell. The ache in my balls became my only reality. I worked to focus on the needs of our passengers, but my mind kept straying to the captain's comments about further instructions. I sat across the aisle from her on the shuttle to the hotel, desperate for some acknowledgment. She never looked in my direction. In the crush at the reception counter, though, she slipped a keycard into my hand. "Four-oh-three. Be there at midnight," she whispered. "And don't be late, Andrew."

That was the beginning. Now all I have to do is see her name on the duty roster and I'm instantly hard. She doesn't use me on every flight, though. Weeks can pass without her summoning me. That only makes me want her more.

When she plans to play with me, she'll greet me as "Andrew" rather than "Mr. Sentosa." And usually, she'll find a way to deliver some devilish item of sexual torture for me to wear throughout the flight: nipple clamps, cock rings, a tight latex jock. Once, on an LAX-Changi run, she gave me a pair of woman's panties, red silk trimmed with black lace. The smooth fabric slithering over my distended prick was just too much. When she handed me her key, I disgraced myself by coming in my pants. She used the cum-drenched garment as a gag while she whipped me.

I couldn't sit down for a week.

Tonight we're en route to Bangkok, and the plug embedded in my ass makes every movement delicious agony. Bending over to place dinner trays on the passengers' tables is particularly tough. Lara, our purser, must have noticed my grimace. She asks if I'm ill. I grin and make some joke about the hazards of foreign food.

It's one in the morning Thai time, ten a.m. in Los Angeles, by the time we check in. I'm exhausted yet wired. The narrow streets around the Montien Hotel are bright with neon and crowded with sweaty, scantily dressed bodies—both tourists and natives. My teak-floored room is shadowed, cool and smells of jasmine. I'd love to lie down, but the captain expects me at her door in half an hour. I'd never disappoint her.

I take a quick shower, avoiding my swollen dick except as necessary to get it clean. I leave the plug in place. I'd given myself an enema before boarding, as Emma had taught me, on the chance that she'd want me on any particular flight. My balls ache when I remember that night in KL, when she first demonstrated her preferred technique. I'd never voided my bowels while someone watched. I wanted to curl up and die of shame. Still, later, when she thrust her latex-sheathed fingers into my raw hole, I came so hard I practically passed out.

I'm at her door one minute before the prescribed time. I wait the required sixty seconds before inserting the key card. The captain cares about punctuality. The delay gives me an opportunity to ponder what she'll do to me tonight. My mind dredges up images so nasty they make me cringe. My erection twitches inside my loose pants. I've been swollen for so long, I can't remember what it feels like not to be hard.

Why am I here? Why do I want this? All-American superstud Andy Sentosa, fraternity president, star quarterback, dream lover and heartbreaker? Why have I placed myself under the thumb of this woman fifteen years older than I am, when I could have a dozen girls, younger and prettier? Why don't I just laugh in her face when she hands me one of her little black bags and tell her to find some other boy to torture?

Because...well, I don't understand why. It has something to do with the authority of her position—the only female pilot flying jumbos for Shambala. It's all tied up with the way she looks right through me, knowing what I fear—and want—before I do myself. For some weird reason, I want to prove to her I can take whatever she'll dish out. I want to please her; to coax out that tight, slightly mocking smile that tells me she's aroused, too.

It's time. The card slides soundlessly into the slot. The LED turns green as the lock clicks. My heart's beating loud enough for me to hear it in my ears. I push the door open and step into her presence.

"Good evening, Andrew." She's seated across the room, in an armchair by the window. I note her position with a quick glance before dropping my eyes to the lush carpet as she likes me to do.

"Good evening, Ma'am." By now I know what's required. I strip off my shirt and pants, fold them—the captain has a thing about neatness—and place them on the desk near the door.

Then I sink to my hands and knees, as gracefully as a gangly six-footer can, and crawl to her across the rug.

When I reach her bare feet, I press a reverent kiss onto each instep. Her skin is baby soft beneath my lips. Her toenails, a natural pink, draw me. I have the urge to lick between her toes, to suck them into my mouth and bathe them in my saliva. I know better, though, than to make that kind of move without being told to do so.

"Good boy," she murmurs. "You may look at me." She's wearing a teal silk robe I've never seen before, belted around the waist and flowing to her ankles. Her unbound hair floats on her shoulders in russet waves. Her face glows with power. I catch a whiff of lilac cologne, and faintly, the low-tide scent of pussy. New blood surges into my already straining cock.

How could I have thought she was plain? Tonight she's a goddess, and I'm privileged to worship her.

"Time for confession, Andrew. It's been nearly two weeks. Who have you screwed since I had you last?"

"No one, Ma'am." It's true. Since Emma Marsden turned her eye in my direction, I haven't really been interested in other women.

"Really? I saw Jennie giving you a look of pure lust when we stopped at Narita. You could have her just by crooking your little finger. You're sure you haven't taken advantage?"

"No, honestly—I've been very good."

Her laughter is like a river dancing over stone. "What about jacking off?"

"Only three times, Ma'am. I'm sorry. I really couldn't help it..."

"Three times in two weeks! You must be exceptionally horny."

Hot blood climbs into my cheeks. "Yes, Captain. I am."

"Stand up. Let me see." Leaning forward, she traces delicate fingers over my rigid dick then clasps me in her palm. I clamp down on the plug, staring at her small hands and struggling for control. "Mmm. Very hard indeed. We'll have to see what we can do about that. But punishment first. You know my rules. You're still wearing the plug?"

"Of course, Ma'am." I try not to whine. Does she really think I would disobey her at this point?

"Excellent. Turn around, Andrew. Nam, come over and help me, please."

My heart nearly leaps out of my chest. I'd thought we were alone. Emma has never invited anyone else to participate in our scenes. But now a tall, willowy Thai beauty rises from the shadowed corner chair where she's been watching the proceedings.

Ebony hair flows almost to the girl's waist. Silver bangles decorate her brown wrists; matching loops shine in her ears. She wears a lot of makeup: gleaming purple eye shadow and dense, probably fake eyelashes. Her purple miniskirt just clears the bottom of her bum and a white, sequin-crusted tank top shows off her dusky cleavage. She smells like the incense the Thais burn in their shrines.

"Suck him, Nam, while I give him his strapping." The exotic creature sinks to her knees with palpable grace and takes me in her slender fingers. My balls tighten; I hang on the edge, knowing that if I come, I'm in for far more severe correction. I'm tempted to let go anyway, to give in and damn the consequences. But that would displease my mistress.

Emma's moving behind me. Something cool and smooth slithers up my back. "My belt," she confirms. "Five strokes for each unauthorized orgasm, or fifteen in all. Count them, Andrew."

Swat! The leather strap lands squarely on my butt, nudging the plug, leaving a dull burn in its wake. At the same moment, the Thai woman swallows my cock. Pleasure streaks to my brain, muddling the hurt.

"One," I manage to croak, as Nam turns on the suction. "Two." This stroke catches the back of my thigh like a lick of flame. Nam's tongue is rough as a cat's, swirling over my knob. Fluid climbs into my shaft, though I try to force it down.

Snap! The belt slashes my shoulder, with yet a different flavor of pain. I arch instinctively, driving down Nam's throat. "Three." How will I survive another twelve lashes? Balanced between ecstasy and agony, only the counting saves me from flying apart. "Four. Five. Six."

Emma pauses to knead my bruised ass and twist the plug. "You're doing well. Hold on now..." Another four strokes, biting into my back, my legs, my buttocks. Nam fondles my balls while sliding her tongue up and down my length. I'm okay now, or so I think, above it all, letting the sensations wash through me without trying to sort them out. "Five more, Andrew," my mistress intones, and I count them automatically, determined not to disappoint the captain no matter what she asks of me.

It's over at last. Nam pulls away as the captain's belt sizzles across my buttcheeks for the last time. I think I'm going to collapse but Emma steps up behind me, the cool silk of her garment soothing my abraded skin. She wraps her arms around my waist. Contentment blooms in my chest. It's all worth it—all the pain, the humiliation, the doubts that attack me when we're apart. This is where I belong.

"Good boy," she murmurs, rubbing her body against my back. She lays her cheek in the hollow between my shoulder blades and licks at one of my stripes. She's so tiny and yet so powerful....

Then something hard emerges from all her softness, prodding the gap between my thighs. My body stiffens—I know what that poking means. She chuckles and steps away, leaving me bereft.

"Of course I brought my harness. Why do you think I wanted you to wear the plug? I need you nice and loose. I plan to fuck you until you scream for mercy. If that's all right with you, that is."

She's already fiddling with the plug. I bow my head in silent assent as she pulls it from my bowels. It emerges with an obscene pop that sends new blood to my prick. I'm ready to explode. I clench my sphincter, gaping after hours of impalement.

"Kneel on the bed, Andrew." She positions me crosswise near the foot, my hands near one edge. "Nam—over here." The Thai woman circles to stand in front of me. Her breasts sparkle under her jeweled shirt. Sweat mingled with sandalwood pricks my nostrils.

Emma sweeps her arm around the girl's shoulder and pulls her into a passionate kiss. Nam has to bend to reach my mistress's mouth. My loins ache, watching—the captain has never kissed me, in all these months. Just as I'm thinking this, she releases the Thai and leans over to brush her lips across mine. It's the briefest of caresses, but I almost moan with joy.

She has discarded her robe. Black straps encircle her waist and thighs, a stark contrast to her pale skin. Her favorite dildo, eight inches long and wreathed with veins, juts from her pubis. She has pulled her hair back from her face. She wears the barest of smiles as she smears lube along the length of her artificial cock.

"Now, Andrew. I'm going to fuck you, as I promised. Meanwhile, I want you to suck Nam. Make her come, and you can come too."

The silent Thai steps forward to within inches of my face and raises the hem of her tiny skirt. She wears nothing underneath. Her pubis is completely hairless. And protruding from that smooth triangle at the top of her tawny thighs is a small but definitely erect penis.

"No!" I scream. The captain's behind me, kneeling on the bed. She holds my hips with impossible strength. "No, please— I can't..."

"Can't, Andrew? Or won't?"

I twist around, away from the freakish sight in front of me, to plead with my mistress. "I'm not gay—don't make me suck his—her—cock. Please, I'll do anything you want..."

"*This* is what I want, Andrew. I thought you liked making me happy. That you enjoyed obeying me." She shrugs and releases her grip. "Very well. Go back to your room then."

Climbing off the bed with an audible sigh, she goes to pick up my clothing from the desk. Nam and I both watch her. I'm entranced by the confident power I see in her neat, muscular body. In a uniform, a silk robe or naked, she was born to command.

Emma tosses my clothes on the bed. "Get dressed. Get out." The coldness in her voice makes me shudder.

"No...wait...I don't want to go."

"Either you obey me, or you leave. I don't have time or patience for this sort of game."

I stare at her stern beauty. How can I leave? I turn back to the miniature erection bobbing obscenely in the Thai's crotch. How can I...?

I swallow the disgust that rises in my throat. "Okay, okay. I'll do it."

"Don't do me any favors, boy."

"Please, Ma'am. Forgive me. Let me suck Nam's cock while you fuck me. I'll do anything—anything to make you happy..."

The ghost of a smile crosses Emma's face, like sun peeking out from behind thunderclouds. "You're sure, boy?"

I nod.

"Well, then..." She resumes her position behind me, her fingers digging into my hips. The slippery tip of her artificial cock presses against my sphincter. "Do it, boy."

I close my eyes and open my mouth. Nam's cock slides between my lips as Emma's drives into my ass.

The dildo's not as thick as the plug—not quite—but considerably longer. The captain wields it without mercy, plunging deep into my bowels with each fierce thrust. Her hips bang against my leather-scarred buttcheeks, adding bright sparks of pain to the richer, darker sensations of being buggered.

The cock in my mouth swells larger as I lap and suck as best I can. Nam's flesh tastes salty and slightly bitter. The musk rising from her groin is nothing like a woman's. Nevertheless, it excites me when she sinks her fingers into my hair and works my mouth up and down over her hardness. My nose bangs against her bare pubis as she strains for release. Saliva streams down my chin until she's soaked. My lips feel bruised and swollen, but she doesn't let up, and neither does the captain.

They fuck me for a long time. I hang in a weird limbo, drunk with the pleasure of being so thoroughly used. *This is who I am*, I realize. *I was born to serve and to obey.* The thought makes me ridiculously happy.

Nam's penis twitches. She moans, the first sound she's uttered all night. A spurt of fluid erupts on my tongue. I force myself to swallow, though my gorge rises in disgust, knowing without being told that this is what my captain requires. More cum floods my mouth. I'm sputtering, choking, drowning in spunk.

Emma rams into me, grinding her pelvis against my ass. A shudder shakes her body and transmits itself to mine. She jerks against me, uttering little cries that I know mean she's reached her peak. I'm so proud, so glad I've done what she asked. I arch back, offering my ass, wanting to give her everything.

She slumps forward, her small breasts mashed against my kidneys. God, she feels good! I'm on the verge of climax myself, but I've been there forever. I can wait, if she wants me to.

But she reaches beneath me to grasp my swollen rod and whispers her permission. I explode at last, spilling my cum all over her small, strong fingers.

We lie on the bed for a sweet space, her body draped across mine. I don't know what's happened to the ladyboy. I drift on the edge of dreams, wanting nothing but to remain there forever. After a while, though, she elbows me in the ribs.

"Get up, Andrew. Time to go back to your room."

Regret stabs at my chest. "Please, Ma'am—let me stay..." She's never allowed me to sleep with her before, but after tonight, perhaps things will change.

"No. Back to your room, right now." She's sitting up beside me, rolling me off the bed and onto the floor.

"Okay, okay. You're the boss." Stiff, my battered flesh protesting, I try to don my pants.

She gives me a satisfied grin. "That's right. I'm glad you haven't forgotten." Her voice mellows. "We have a two-day layover here in Bangkok, you know. I'm shopping tomorrow, and having dinner with friends in the evening, but perhaps after that you'll join me."

"I'd like that, Ma'am." I'm sure she hears the raw need in my voice. I don't care.

"Perhaps I'll have Nam back, have her fuck you. Or have you fuck her. Get you over your little homophobic qualms..."

A sickish thrill runs through me. My cock starts to harden.

"Whatever you say, Captain."

JUICY TIDBITS

Dominic Santi

I 've spent most of my life in front of a camera. When my latest movie went blockbuster, though, I went from twenty-six-year-old, starving actor to "instant" stardom. Every time I saw my face on a fast-food drink, I did a double take. When I almost hit a parked car, gawking at my image on a downtown billboard, my agent/business manager/girlfriend took my car keys and pulled me over her lap for another intense session on how to deal with the media.

I looked just enough different without makeup and hair extensions that I wasn't recognized in public as often as many stars. But as the ongoing PR blitz intensified, Christie said that would change. She knew how nervous I got doing live publicity. We practiced potential questions and answers until I rarely blurted out what Christie called the private *juicy tidbits* that sent the media hounds diving for their cell phones.

The talk-show host caught me off guard. Taping for that night's program was going smoothly. We'd gone to commercial.

I relaxed when the red light on the camera stopped blinking. The cameraman was stretching next to his equipment, drinking his coffee. I'd pretty much forgotten about the studio audience. Jared leaned toward me and said he was going to need something stronger than coffee after the show. His house had been full of repairmen since dawn, when his washing machine had flooded the downstairs. He told me he was even going commando because of the laundry crisis. He winked and said that reminded him—he'd need to ask me a "boxers or briefs?" teaser when we went back to taping.

I laughed and told him not to waste his time. "I don't even own underwear!"

He raised his eyebrows. "Can't you afford underwear now?"

I told him, "Well, duh! Yeah!" But, I explained, I was too much of a slob to deal with more than the bare minimum of laundry. He eyed me up and down. I was wearing black jeans and a black silk shirt. He told me even though silk was high maintenance, I didn't look too shabby.

I laughed again. "That's just the wardrobe people." Then I went on to tell him about the time last winter when my landlady unexpectedly stopped by. Filming had just wrapped up for the movie. My roommate's even worse than I am about cleaning, and I was busy auditioning for another part. As usual, the housework was such a low priority, it hadn't even made my To Do list.

"Mrs. Johnson near dropped her teeth! There were dirty dishes everywhere—in the sink, on the counters, even piled on the stove. We had gnats, for godsake!" I rolled my eyes, feeling my face flush as I added. "She grabbed the one clean wooden spoon in the dish drainer and blistered my butt right there in the kitchen!"

"Your landlady spanks you?"

Fuck, oh fuck! The red light on the camera was blinking again!

"You're an internationally famous movie star, an adult who's lived on his own for years, and your landlady walks into your house unannounced and *spanks* you for not doing the dishes? Ladies and gentlemen, we need to talk about this!"

We sure as fuck did not! But that asshole had a one-track mind, and he'd steered me into what we both knew was one juicy exclusive. I used every trick my flustered mind could remember, but this was one scenario Christie and I definitely hadn't practiced. Even I couldn't believe I'd blurted that out!

No, I wasn't being abused. I had no comments about whether or not I advocated corporal punishment. My being spanked had nothing to do with my acting skills—or with the movie! Mrs. Johnson was *not* a monster! She was pissed about the unsanitary kitchen, which I knew better than to have. Shit, it wasn't like we hadn't done that song and dance before. I'm a slob!

That set off a whole new round of questions. By the time the interview finally ended, my head was throbbing. It would be hours before the show aired, but there was already a swarm of reporters at the stage door. As I ducked the flashes and dove into Christie's car, I was ready to choke that son of a bitch!

And I was so pissed at myself, I could hardly see straight. Christie's vision of being my agent had included a full course of bodyguard training, so it wasn't long before she'd lost the chase cars in traffic.

"I cannot fucking believe this!" I thumped against the seat so hard my head banged the headrest. "That asshole set me up!"

"Language."

Christie's voice was low and firm. I glanced quickly as she downshifted around a curve. We were climbing into the foothills, away from the city. Her long, dark hair flowed over her shoulder in the afternoon sunlight.

"Sorry," I muttered, running my hand through my hair. "That *jerk* set me up. I'm still pi—um, I mean, ticked off."

"Better." She smiled and hit the switch for the electric windows. A cool breeze blew in over my face. I shut up and took deep, calming breaths. The air cleared as we rose above the smog. We wound past a dense stand of trees, then turned onto the road that ran to our favorite parking place, overlooking the city. It was far enough into the mountains to be surrounded by woods with only the sun-filled sky above us. I'd never been there in the daytime before. When we reached the final turnoff, Christie left the main road, following an unpaved track until we came out onto the lookout. She pulled over, parked, and we both got out.

"No point in going home. The place is going to be swamped with reporters."

I slapped my hand against my forehead. My roommate was going to be pissed as hell about that, especially if the ruckus got in the way of any auditions. But we'd shared rent since we first came to town, and he was one of my closest friends. I had no doubt he'd tell the locusts to fuck off. He'd be laughing his ass off, though. He thought it was hilarious when the paddle came out and my pants went down because of the housekeeping. He put on earphones to drown out my yells, and a couple of hours later, he was enjoying the lemony fresh scent of living in a sparkling clean environment.

He also wouldn't tell the media that for the past six months, the spankings had become so frequent that our environment was clean most of the time now. It wasn't my landlady swinging the paddle anymore.

Christie had moved in with us. I was shit-faced in love with her. I wanted this relationship to last, so I'd also taken a deep breath and admitted that, try as I might, when it came to my living circumstances, I was one of the most irresponsible people on earth.

Christie had responsibility down pat. After two hours of negotiating who would do what chores and when, I'd finally suggested hiring a fulltime housekeeper. One look at her raised eyebrows had me adding, "Or not."

"Not" won. Even if Christie hadn't already invested my earnings for me and put me on a strict but generous allowance, she felt it was high time I learned a modicum of responsibility. In the end, she decided the three of us would split the cost of a housekeeper twice a week to clean the common areas and bathrooms. We would each be responsible for keeping our personal space clean. And I was in charge of kitchen cleanup.

Since Christie was a kick-ass cook, I was fine with having meals at home every night. I was amazed at how much more energy I had when I cut out fast-food dinners and started getting enough sleep. Going to bed early was easy with Christie waiting between my sheets.

It took the better part of a month and damn near daily paddlings, though, for me to realize that if I wanted to eat sitting down again, or sleep in any position but on my belly, I was going to have to remember, all on my own, to do the dishes after dinner—every single night. The day after we negotiated the household rules, Christie had taken Mrs. Johnson and me to lunch at a secluded restaurant on the other side of town. Three Cobb salads and a carafe of chardonnay later, Mrs. Johnson had ceremoniously taken her "traveling" paddle from her purse and handed it to Christie while I frantically looked around to be sure nobody was watching.

That night, when I chose playing video games over doing the

dishes, Christie had broken the paddle in. Across my butt. Bare, just the way Mrs. Johnson always had. When I finally stopped bawling, I did the dishes wearing just my T-shirt and my socks. My asshole roommate didn't even blink when he walked in to get a beer from the refrigerator, though I'm pretty sure I heard him snicker when I looked back at the dishes.

I didn't give a shit. Christie was happy that I was finally becoming responsible. She still routinely paddled the hell out of my butt for the zillion other jackass things I did. But I'd gotten comfortable with her being in charge of both my personal and professional life. Things had never gone more smoothly—or more lucratively.

And I loved the way she let me fuck her until she screamed, every single night. It didn't matter whether or not my backside was on fire, or if I was still sniffling from a paddling. When she grabbed my butt and pulled me deep into her, I came so hard I nearly passed out.

"Gnats in the kitchen." She laughed now as she scrubbed her hands over her face. "I don't know if you're ever going to live that down, babe." Her eyes sparkled as she grinned at me. "And a bare-bottom paddling from your irate landlady."

"I didn't tell him it was bare," I grouched. Damn, Christie was pretty. It was hard to stay grumpy as I watched her walk over to me. She wrapped her arms around me. Sighing, I held her close and rested my face in her hair. "I've never been so embarrassed in my life."

"Not even the first time you took down your pants for me to paddle you?"

I shivered as her fingers stroked down my backside. "Close."

"I liked that you didn't have underwear on. With one snap of my fingers, your jeans were at your knees, and your gorgeous, round butt was bent over the counter."

Actually, it hadn't been a finger snap. She'd smacked the paddle on her palm and told me I had to the count of three to get my backside as bare as the day I was born. Even with buttons, I'd made it.

"I have to admit, it was hard spanking you that first time. Your bottom was so red and hot, and you were crying so hard and dancing against the counter. If Mrs. Johnson hadn't convinced me how much you needed your spankings to be butt burners, I would have stopped long before then. That wouldn't have done you any good at all."

I leaned back fast and looked at her. "You don't have to spank me hard, you know. Just a few taps would probably do the trick—over my jeans. OW!"

Her brows were lifted straight up, but her eyes were twinkling. "Or not."

"OW! Or not!" My butt stung where she smacked it once more. "Okay. Probably not." I hissed with each of the next half-dozen swats. "All right. I need my butt paddled hard to get anything through my hard head."

"I know." She wiggled against me, rubbing her belly over my shaft. My cock was filling fast. "I also know you're going to keep kicking yourself for letting that jerk trick you into giving him his juicy tidbit to twist around for tonight's headlines." Her fingers settled firmly on the lower curve of my bottom. I shivered.

"You're not going to let go of this without a spanking, are you?"

I wanted to say yes, but I was shaking my head, even as my face heated. "No, Ma'am." I could get over being mad at other people. When I got mad at myself, though, I stayed mad.

"Bare your bottom and lean over the car. You have to the count of three."

I was glad she didn't give me time to think before a spanking. I marched over to the car, unbuttoning my pants and shoving them down as she rummaged through her purse. By the time she had the paddle in her hand, I was at the side of the car, bending over the trunk. Her hand rested firmly on the small of my back.

"OW!" Damn, that first swat stung!

The rest were every bit as bad. Christie paddled up one side of my butt and down the other, setting every square inch of my poor, sore, sensitive flesh on fire while I bawled and danced and pressed my hands into the warm, smooth metal. When she finally stopped, I jumped up, hiccupping and clutching my butt.

"Hands on your head."

"Yes, M-ma'am." It was a good thing the taping was over for the day, because the makeup artist would have been working overtime to get my face presentable. Spankings are cathartic for me, and I don't cry gracefully. I was a mess.

Christie's fingers trailed softly down the side of my face. "Better?"

It was hard to see her through my tears, but I nodded and hiccupped again. "My butt hurts, Christie. It hurts bad."

"I know, baby." Her kisses peppered my cheeks as she slid up onto the car. Oh, damn. She had her pants off. They hung from one ankle as she put her hands on my waist and pulled me to her. My cock had softened from the spanking, but in the time it took her to wrap her legs around my waist, I was rock hard all over again. She had a condom in her hands. I groaned as she rolled it on.

"Inside me, babe. Your spanking's over now. I want a good, hard fuck."

I gave her one. I gave us both one. I fucked her until her teeth rattled, or maybe mine did. I came so hard I shouted. I didn't give a fuck if the evening news chopper was flying overhead. *Thank god it wasn't.* The squirrels that saw my bright-red ass bucking into her on the side of a car in broad daylight kept their mouths on their acorns and ignored us.

The drive back down the mountain was uncomfortable as hell. Christie drove again, because the only thing on my mind was keeping my weight off my sore, hot ass. A call to our roommate let us know he was playing serious mind games with the TV trucks in the driveway. He'd hung a Ping-Pong paddle emblazoned with the words FUCK YOU in the living room window.

I couldn't wait to see what kind of a PR spin Christie was going to put on that juicy tidbit.

HER MAJESTY'S PLAYTHING

Lawrence Westerman

1

The kiss of her whip is not a punishment but a reward. The patient waiting, the juggling of schedules, the mounting anticipation, all culminate in a transcendent, sublime crescendo when he's groveling on the carpet at her feet.

Her whip is heavy; a short, thick lash of braided black leather. It whooshes through the air and cuts deeply into his flesh. He kneels naked before her, holding still by force of will without the benefit of bondage to keep him in place.

Her whip is a weapon to be feared. She could break him in a matter of seconds if she chose to. She builds the tempo slowly, painting angry red stripes on his pale skin. She whips him with vigor, concentrating on a single area at a time. Deep purple bruises appear within the swaths of vivid crimson. He kisses and licks her elegant black stilettos, sucking on the impossibly high heels.

He does not cry out but breathes deeply. It is cold in the room but he begins to sweat. The chemistry in his body is changing. His endorphins kick in as the ferocity of the whipping increases, allowing him to ride the waves of sensation. He surrenders to her absolutely and sinks deep into the promised land of submission.

In the beginning he is unsure he will be able to withstand her onslaught. By the end he wants it to go on forever. He accepts every cut with gratitude. He is stoned, high as a kite. He belongs to her completely and irrevocably. "Thank you, Ma'am," he stammers earnestly with every stroke of the lash.

"Don't thank me. Just be quiet and take your punishment! I don't want to hear anything from you," she replies sternly. He feels her stiletto heel on the back of his neck pushing his face into the carpet. He lets out a muffled whimper.

Finally his whipping is over. He drifts for a few precious moments, quietly recovering at her feet. Without warning she cuts him with three ferocious strokes. Her attack is unexpected. He cries out in pain and surprise. "What are you crying about?" she says with playful mockery, lashing him again.

He kneels, head bowed, ass in the air like a Muslim in prayer. She dons a pair of rubber gloves. He hears the sound of air escaping the lubricant bottle as she squeezes the viscous liquid onto her fingers. She pushes a finger inside him. He is relaxed and willing. Two fingers slip in. She is exploring him, making him slippery and wet.

She presses the toy against him gently but insistently. Instinctively he shuts it out. It feels huge. She pushes again, careful but determined. For a moment he doubts himself.

He wills himself to relax and open up to her like a flower. There is a momentary twinge of pain as the head slips inside. This is the moment he has been waiting for. The moment he has been dreaming of. He wants to loop this feeling and put it on infinite repeat.

She pushes her cock inside of him slowly, inexorably. It feels deliciously thick. She lets him kneel there for a minute savoring the sensation. She turns up the rotary dial at the base. He feels the vibrations commence. She pulls it all the way out and slides it back in. He groans in a paroxysm of ecstatic submission. She explores him deeply and thoroughly, sliding it in up to the hilt. He submits to her completely. She fucks him with a slow, regular rhythm, impaling him again and again. He wants her to rip him apart. She is gentle but determined. He thanks her earnestly. He pleads with her to fuck him harder. He begs to be her bitch.

She gives him permission to come, reaching between his legs and taking his balls in her rubber-gloved fingers. He trembles and buries his face in the rug. She continues to sodomize him, milking the orgasm from him tenderly, expertly. He groans deliriously, spilling over the edge into unmitigated bliss. He slowly floats back to earth overwhelmed by a feeling of gratitude.

Later he stares at himself in the mirror, gazing in rapt fascination at the marks of her lash. His flesh feels hot. He runs his fingers over the raised welts. Clearly delineated stripes of angry red become treasured souvenirs that will fade all too soon; lipstick traces left behind by the kiss of her terrible, beautiful whip.

The next day he is extraordinarily happy and relaxed. On the way home from work he buys her a dozen red roses. He is so thankful to belong to her—grateful to be Her Majesty's plaything.

2

Her Majesty is a generous monarch. She gives her plaything gifts beyond his wildest dreams. It is a raw, cold, rainy afternoon. They spend it indoors recovering from a day of Christmas shopping (her) and household chores (him). She sits on the couch watching television. He lies beneath her on the floor. She uses his face as her footstool, teasing him mercilessly with her toes and the soles of her feet.

His scheduled orgasm has been postponed due to their hectic schedule. She is feeling happy and relaxed. It seems like the perfect opportunity to ask her for something he deeply desires. Finally he gets up the nerve to ask her if they can try something new. She listens to his suggestion and smiles warmly.

Later that evening he wrestles valiantly with the testicle parachute. It seems impossibly tight, but he finally manages to get it on. He attaches the penis bands to his cock. He watches her slide a pair of sheer black stockings up her beautiful legs. He hands her the remote control and lies beneath her on the floor. She adjusts the channels on the electro-stimulation device then switches the mode to WAVES. She places her left foot over his nose and mouth. The toes of her right foot frolic playfully in his pubic hair. She turns the juice up very slowly.

In WAVES mode the electric shock starts as a barely perceptible whisper, builds to a crescendo then dissipates. It feels like a tingling wave of pleasure rolling in from the distant horizon and crashing on the shore. As she gradually turns up the power the crest of each wave becomes increasingly powerful. He can't wait for the next wave to come rolling in. He is helpless to speed up his orgasm. He is completely under her control.

He ardently kisses her toes and the bottoms of her feet. He watches the look of amused concentration on her face as she adjusts the controls. She is far above him and deciding his fate. The waves are breaking with ever-increasing intensity. He wonders what level the device is on. He cannot see the digital readout. The pain is delicious. He wants more. Nothing matters but her nylon-covered feet and the waves breaking incessantly on the shore.

Without warning he spurts onto her nylons. Seconds later

another explosion erupts onto his belly and chest. Each crescendo of current triggers a geyser he is helpless to control. His orgasm is milked from him in a slow, exquisite dance.

He sighs, looking up at her in wonder. He is elated and intensely grateful. "Your balls are purple!" she exclaims with laughter, as he removes the testicle parachute.

3

He sits at his desk staring listlessly out the window then back at his computer screen. It is afternoon and the hectic buzz of the workday has been reduced to a lifeless crawl. His mind drifts. He imagines kneeling at her feet as she brings up the current. Suddenly he is filled with impatience and longs to be home with her. It feels like the workday will never end.

When he arrives the house is empty. Only the cat greets him, purring and rubbing against his ankles. She arrives just after him. She has been at jury duty all week: some fraud case involving an old woman stealing thousands from a country club. He helps her remove her boots. The weather has been horrible: rain, sleet, snow and frozen drizzle.

She tells him she has been feeling slightly depressed and under the weather lately. She has been feeling fat and unattractive. He holds her close and reassures her that he loves her regardless of a few extra pounds. She smiles at him and gives him a kiss. "I am very lucky to have you," she says.

She asks him to pour her a glass of wine while she returns a call to her sister. She reclines on the couch, sipping her wine and chatting on the phone. He lies on the floor beneath her. He removes her slippers and gives her a foot rub, taking little breaks to kiss the bottoms of her feet and suck on her toes. She absentmindedly runs her fingers through his hair, as he passionately worships her feet. She caresses his face with the soles of her feet and slides her toes into his mouth. He is oozing into his shorts. Their son is expected home any minute but he is reaching a peak of desperation. What to do?

When she gets off the phone, he asks for permission to come. She looks down at his cock jutting shamelessly from his boxers and laughs. "Would you like me to sit on your face?" she asks with a wicked smile.

"Oh, yes, Ma'am! Oh, please, Ma'am!" he replies almost breathlessly. His BlackBerry vibrates. Their son is at a café concert and will be home late. Eagerly he follows her upstairs to the bedroom.

He hurriedly strips off his clothes. She kneels over his head and removes her panties. Slowly she lowers herself onto his face. He breathes in her delicious aroma and kisses the inside of her thighs. He gently probes her with his tongue. He finds the precious little bud that awaits him and explores the sensitive cleft just beneath the hood. She groans and grabs him by the hair. She holds his head in place until she is finished. Reversing position, she sits full on his face driving his tongue all the way inside of her. She tastes tart and bitter. He licks eagerly. He is hypnotized by the sight of her above him.

Only she exists in his world. He wants this moment to last forever. He would happily die beneath her. She tenderly squeezes his balls. He shudders and erupts. It is always over too soon. She looks down at him and smiles. He watches longingly as she rises from his face and slips her panties back on. He was born to be Her Majesty's throne.

4

They renew their wedding vows in front of a small gathering. She puts him in charge of the catering, which stresses him out. In the end everything works out fine. The guests are served hors d'oeuvres. He kneels at her feet and promises to honor and obey her until the end of his days. Her Majesty lovingly places a slave collar around his neck and plants a kiss on his forehead. He reverently kisses the toes of her black leather boots.

Most of their friends realize that she *calls the shots* in their relationship. There was never much doubt who *wore the pants*. Their female friends sometimes remark how *well behaved* or *well trained* he is. With this deeply symbolic ceremony everything is finally out in the open.

Now they are entering a new phase. As he kneels before her, he once again becomes aware of the chastity device restraining his cock. He gazes at the key hanging from a gold chain around her neck. A delicious sinking feeling in the pit of his stomach reminds him that he is completely under her control. He lovingly pours her a glass of champagne and goes to fetch her something to eat.

"You are so lucky," one of the female guests exclaims. "I would love to have my husband cater to my every whim like your husband does for you! I'm not sure I could ask him to do something like this though. I would feel like he was somehow less of a man; as though I had symbolically castrated him on some level."

"My darling has a slavish heart," Her Majesty responds with a smile. "Believe me, he's happier this way."

He returns with her food. Bending down on one knee he hands her the plate, looking up at her with adoration.

"Sweetheart, what makes you the happiest man in the world?"

"Belonging to you and serving you, Ma'am!" he replies without hesitation.

"You see?" she says, smiling and taking a sip of champagne.

BOTTLED
AND BOUND

Jacqueline Brocker

And then, just seconds after James had eased drops of massage oil onto his palm, the bottle slipped and vanished into the bath water with a heavy plop.

Regina glared into the mirror in front of the tub, meeting James's horrified expression in its reflection.

"Well, get it out!" she snapped.

While he fished in the warm, lilac-scented water, chanting over and over how sorry he was, Regina sighed, disappointed. So very disappointed.

Her expression didn't reveal the strange delight that was rising within her.

James had done everything right that evening. The key word she had texted after she finished work, *Shattered*, had told him what she expected. She'd come home to a house decked in candlelight, to have James remove her coat and heels and store them in the correct places, to devour a sumptuous repast rich with cream and tomato and imbibe the two glasses of sparkling wine James had poured her. Afterward, he'd offered her his arm and brought her upstairs to the bathroom, steamy with hot mist, all white marble and gilded edges and in pride of place the long bathtub with curled, gold lion's paws. He'd undressed her, and pointedly ignored her nakedness, even as his cock was clearly half-hard through his black jeans, and hadn't touched her but to help her into the tub. Regina had sunk back into the water, scented just as she knew it would be, and relaxed for a good long while, knowing that James would be sitting on the stool, waiting for her to request a massage.

Ever since the day, a year and a half ago, that James had rescued her dropped handbag from the escalators at the nearest tube station, he had been willing to do anything for her.

"Anything?" Regina had asked on their third date.

"Yes." His answer was utterly sincere.

Still, Regina had been surprised when he'd agreed to her exact terms. Very pleased, though. He was distinctly attractive, with fine cheekbones and a striking profile, and the pale brown hair that would always suggest boyishness. *Lucky to find him* didn't begin to cover it.

It had taken her a year to teach him how she wanted her house run, how she liked her meals, how she needed her clothes ironed. James adjusted his schedule to work mostly from home, so he had time to do as she expected. As good as he was, he had also learned the hard way that variations or forgetfulness would earn him a swift punishment.

So too would clumsiness.

She had trained him well, so well that even though her eyes were closed, his hands would not stray to his cock and stroke it through his jeans. Regina had thought, though, that he would have known that resting something on the lip of the bathtub was a stupid thing to do. Apparently not.

The massage was one of her favorite parts of this ritual. And now, the bottle—a decidedly expensive bottle—was spilling its contents into the bathwater. He was still babbling his apologies when he drew it out and tried to shake the water out of it.

"Shut up."

The steam itself stilled as James froze, meeting Regina's eyes in the mirror. She straightened up, still glaring at him, and said:

"Finish what you started. We'll continue as usual and look to your punishment after."

James nodded. "Yes, M'lady."

M'lady. It had taken him a long time to say it without awkwardness; now it flowed with the natural ease of a knight's tribute.

He reapplied the oil to his palms—this time putting the bottle down on the floor. The massage was competent, but the tense anticipation of what she would do later permeated each touch and squeeze. His face was full of concentration, and his breaths were juddering.

Regina relished that, her lips curling in the mirror, parting as if she could taste his fear.

Later, after he patted her dry, he led her to the bedroom. As she lay back on the blue satin pillows and cover of the canopied bed, velvet drapes either side of her, she gazed over James's shoulder—for he was to remain standing until she told him otherwise—to the far end, where the leather-covered saltire cross stood. Next to that was another leather bench, and a large mahogany chest decorated with sharp studs. James, standing with his back to them, must have been aware of what she was looking at, and thinking, and he bit his lip, cheeks blooming red.

Well, he still had some time before his punishment, Regina thought.

Regina eased back, parting her knees with her hands, slowly revealing her cunt to James. James's hands clenched by his side as she brushed two fingers down her neck and across her collarbone.

"Your little mishap aside, it was a lovely bath, James." Regina's fingers found a nipple, brushing down it once, then back up again three more times.

James nodded, chest beginning to rise and fall. "Thank you, M'lady."

Regina smiled. She gave the nipple a small pinch and twist, and skirted over her ribs and stomach to the sculpted pubic hair. Just before she found her clit, the path diverted to trace a line down her inner thigh. James's head twitched, and he clasped his hands behind his back. She drew one finger back up, spreading her labia, opening herself so he could see the wet beginnings of her desire. His breathing quickened, and his erection expanded beneath the denim. Regina could have sunk her teeth right into it, if she'd had a mind to.

"Do you want to touch me, James?"

"Yes, M'lady," he answered, voice husky. "I want to worship you."

"With what?"

"With everything."

Her chest swelled with desire; she could have let him have her right then and there, but instead she said, "Let's start with your hands and mouth."

James removed his shirt, fingers trembling. Not surprising; it had been at least two weeks since she had let him worship, allowing his hands only on her back for massage, to embrace her when they were both clothed in nightwear for bed, or in the mornings before she went to work. She had ridden *him*, of course—straddling him, penetrating him—but his hands had been bound on those occasions. She supposed she should not even be allowing him to do this, as part of the punishment, but this was for her now as much as him; she'd been craving his mouth and hands all day.

James's lips—thin and agile—caressed the length of her body, toe to neck, leaving trails of saliva and burning lust all over her. His fingers stroked her skin as if brushing her hair, never probing or pressing, and while he edged very close, he never touched her cunt, though it was becoming wet and plump and Regina was beginning to pant; he would get into deep trouble if he did so before she said.

By the time his mouth was latched to one nipple, his fingers rolling the other, Regina couldn't stop from throwing her head back and moaning. *So well trained,* she thought. God, he'd learned to please her magnificently.

James brought his head up. "Please, M'lady, please...let me worship you better. Please..."

She grabbed his chin and pressed her mouth to his ear. "Do you think you have any right to ask anything of me after your mistake?"

He shook his head, looking down abashed. "No, M'lady."

Regina let go and traced her fingers down his taut cheek. "Lucky for you, I'm ready."

James grinned like a pleased boy, arched down, gave each nipple a kiss, and traced his tongue all the way down her center line, through her pubic hair, brushing over her clit, then lips. Regina grinned, then sighed as, carefully, he slipped two fingers into her very wet cunt, cupping one hand to her breast, and placed his mouth like a delicious padlock over her clit.

His fingers inside her were dexterous, as always, as was his hand, grasping one breast then the other, switching to drive her mad. He was an expert with his tongue and sucking mouth, knowing when to go rapidly, then slowly, then faster still. Yes, she thought. This was pure worship. Divine sensations coursed through her body, James pressing deep, long and insistent, until orgasm overtook her, and she cried out, clutching his head to her cunt, his tongue lapping at her pulsing clit, eliciting smaller, sharper shots of pleasure with each new press.

When she was done, panting still, James raised his head and smiled, pleased. He hoped, she knew, that in her ecstasy she would have forgotten his punishment.

James was always too optimistic.

Regina sat up, still recovering with heavy breaths, and looked James right in the eye. "Bring me the black robe."

James gazed at her imploringly. The black robe meant that the punishment would be a serious one. Regina snapped her fingers in the direction of her clothes cupboard.

"Now."

James sighed and did as she asked. Regina stood, and he draped the black silk over her shoulders, allowing her to slip her arms down the long sleeves; loving how it slithered against her naked, hot body; how it fluttered around her calves and across the back of her ankles. James tied it at the waist for her, hands trembling once more.

Regina smirked and adjusted the robe to her a little. She pointed to the leather-bound cross at the other end of the room.

"Stand in front of it with your hands behind your back."

James walked the length of the room, the tension keeping his shoulders back and his neck straight. When he stood at attention as she commanded, his breathing became ragged.

Regina made him wait for nearly two minutes before she approached him. He was magnificently ready for punishment: his lean, sculpted physique; the smoothness of his skin—she'd ordered him to keep hairless; the bulging erection. The whole package of him taut with preparation for the pain that was about to come.

When she stood level with him, she let her lip curl up as he took a deep breath, his eyes trying to avoid hers. Regina sniggered, and sharply pulled the buttons of his jeans open, yanking them down to his knees. His cock fell forward, bouncing as he moaned. She didn't touch it, but licked her lip as she gave it a hard stare. Long, turgid and with a drop of pearly precum on the head.

"You're a very naughty boy, James, to have such a hard dick."

His cheeks flushed, and he closed his eyes, casting his head down. "You're very beautiful, M'lady."

"Look at me when you speak!"

His eyes flicked up and met hers. His fear was so palpable, she could almost bite it.

"That's better. Now," she said, grabbing his cock and twisting it just a little, so he hissed through his teeth, "take your jeans all the way off, and stand so I can tie you to the cross."

"Yes, M'lady."

When he was naked, his arms and legs stretched out in front of the cross, Regina went to the mahogany chest. From out of it she took four black velvet cords, and, after some deliberation, the riding crop. Behind her, James whimpered. Regina shivered in response.

Quickly, she tied his wrists and ankles, making sure his body was taut. James's ribs rose and fell with increased rapidity, and by the time she was done, his eyes were full of terror and panic.

He started to whisper, "Please, M'lady, I'm so sorry—"

"Shut up!" Regina snapped the riding crop down onto one thigh, and James gasped.

"Oh, god…"

She hit his other thigh, and he yelped.

"From now on, no talking unless I ask you something. Understand?"

James nodded, pressing his lips tightly together.

"Good. Now…do you recall how much that bottle of oil cost?"

"It was…forty pounds, M'lady."

"Forty." Regina laid the tip of the crop on one of James's nipples, pressing against it. James's eyes looked down at it, and she shot the crop under his chin, forcing his face back up.

"That's a lot of money. It was lovely oil too. And you went and wasted it through your clumsiness."

"M'lady—ah!"

Right against his chest. "No talking! Right. For that disobedience, there will be five strikes. And for the bottle of oil…forty. Actually, no. Forty pounds was what it cost us, but that doesn't account for the hours of lost pleasure." She traced the tip of the crop from his chin to his throat, down his chest, and followed the path all the way down the length of his leaking cock. "Let's say eighty. So eighty-five in total."

James made a sound like a crying owl. His whole body shook. His cock bobbed, making the crop rise and fall. It was a harsh punishment, and Regina loved how his fingers flexed, how his body was already bracing for the strikes, his sinewy muscles tightening, both scared and wanting it at once, she knew.

"My only mercy is that the last ten will be on your cock. I will not hit it before then. Of course, you're not to come until I tell you. Understood?"

"Yes, M'lady."

"Good."

He could move so little on the cross. Only twitch, and tense, and turn his head away, desperate to brace himself against the pain she delivered. Regina knew eighty-five was a lot, but it meant she had so many strikes to play with, and his whole body, except for his cock, to give it to.

The first ten were struck at random—biceps, chest, hips, inner thigh—not hard, the warm-up necessary. So were the next five, after which Regina paused, running the crop down James's quivering sides, all the way to his shin.

Five blows there, where bone lay just under the skin. James screamed, torture-pitched sounds. By now, Regina knew, his body would be buzzing from the pain, not wanting to accept it, trying to deny it, but desperately craving it too. And there were fifty-five strikes to go before she touched his cock.

She swapped ten between the tender parts of his inner thighs, avoiding his swelling balls. He tried to bow his legs, knees buckling outward, but he could not escape her fierce attention.

Regina began to growl, lashing at him once more at random. The smacking sounds of leather on skin, James's strangled voice trying not to sob, made a wonderful cacophony in her ears, with the sight of him trying, but failing, to twist away; his stomach and rib cage contracting, the spots of red blooming on his skin, a stunning vision. He was taking his punishment so well, trying to stay controlled, not quite able to manage it. Her already wet cunt was streaming once more, and she was so tempted to throw the crop aside and just ride his cock to orgasm, but she had to teach him this lesson or she would render the relationship useless.

It was when she started at his nipples that tears began rolling down his face. James's lips moved between taut and slack, his head lolled. Regina could not tell if he'd been counting them, but to her vague disappointment, they were almost done.

Just the last ten to go.

"That's seventy-five. You remember what I said about not coming?"

"Yes, M'lady," James said, his voice tremulous through his weeping.

"Good." Regina stepped back, far enough that she could reach the lower end of the crop to the top of James's almost purple cock.

Regina raised the crop. "Count them for me."

James nodded, and before he could brace himself, Regina made the first strike.

He gasped. "One!"

His cock bobbed up and down. Regina brought the crop back up, catching the head, totally free of the foreskin. He jerked and cried out, "Two!"

Three, four, five, to the left, right, and left—swift and shocking. James barely coughed out, "Five…" squeezing his eyes tight before opening them to a fresh spill of tears.

Six was right in the center of his shaft, and *seven* a harsh upward flick. James could only whisper, "Seven…" and he inhaled with shuddering breath. His eyes were red and wet; there was a bright line of tears down each of his cheeks. And his cock was ready to burst.

Regina raised the crop for the last three, meeting his eyes, waiting for him to compose himself. He saw what she was doing, and raised his chin up, inhaling a bracing breath, and nodded.

She spoke the counts with him. *Eight!* Firm with a single beat between each. *Nine!* They all landed in the same spot, the corona where shaft met head. And at last with *Ten!* James sobbed, letting himself openly weep as he hadn't before.

Regina let go of the crop, ignoring its clatter to the ground as she went to him and cradled his head, kissing his cheek repeatedly, running soothing hands down his chest.

"Have you learned your lesson?"

James nodded into her neck, and between sobs said, "Yes, M'lady."

She kissed his temple, and pulled back, wiping his tears away. "Okay. Anything I do to you now, you're allowed to come."

Despite her own slickness, Regina crouched. With a careful pinch using thumb and forefinger, she guided his rock-hard length between her lips, and sucked three times.

It was enough to make him scream and shoot everything he had into her mouth. He coated the back of her tongue with his hot semen, and she swallowed, continuing to suck as a second then third spurt spilled into her, his cries echoing around them. He tasted so good, the sticky, salty, maleness of him, a delight after all she had made him do, all she had done to him. So sexy, so delicious and all hers.

Regina stood. There was a single drop of cum left on her lips, so she leaned forward, and without her asking him to, even as he was panting still, he kissed it away.

She ran her nails through his hair, feeling his pulse through his scalp. "Now, what do we say?"

James smiled shakily. "I love you, M'lady."

Regina's face began to falter, but she tightened herself, keeping stern as she laughed as one would at a child. "That's lovely, but it's not what I meant."

James smiled. "Thank you for teaching me my lesson, and for making me come, M'lady."

Regina kissed him again and began to untie the ropes; she said in his ear: "And I love you. Just learn to be more careful next time."

RED DELICIOUS

Leela Scott

The stale air of Sterling Hall, room 206, was suffocating. The breath of seventy other undergrads hung in the open space, taking over until there wasn't a pure molecule left to be inhaled. Just thinking about the moist, reused air rushing out of her fellow students' mouths, onto the back of her neck and into her hair made the remnants of last night's tequila make a reappearance. It had taken all of Chelsea's willpower to ignore the churning of her hungover stomach and come to class that morning. She didn't really have much of a choice; Professor Stevens would ream her if she missed another lecture.

The shoddy air-conditioning system was down again, leaving the nearly windowless room warm and muggy in the September heat. The thin cotton dress she had thrown on in her rush to make it to class in time stuck to her glistening skin as she struggled to keep up with the professor's endless stream of notes.

"*Legend of Good Women* is a hybrid text. Unlike some of

his earlier works, this text is not simply a dream vision; Chaucer also employs the use of a framed narrative, an embedded ballad and a legendary..." Professor Stevens's velvety smooth voice sounded above the low din of the lecture hall. She stood at her post behind the rickety wooden podium. Despite the poor quality of the venue, she still exuded a power and grace that rivaled any Ivy League lecturer or other woman of prestige. With her chestnut hair swooped up in an intricate twist and deep-rose lipstick accentuating her full mouth, Professor Kayla Stevens commanded attention.

Chelsea squirmed in her seat, the backs of her legs sticking to the hard plastic chair slick with sweat. She pulled her copy of *The Collected Works of Chaucer* out of her bag and frantically tried to find the prologue of the poem Professor Stevens had begun reading. She would be completely lost with no hope of catching up if she didn't follow along word for word as the professor sped through the Middle English text. Despite her best efforts, Chelsea couldn't even find the right work, let alone the prologue. Trying to follow by ear, she became entranced by the melodic rise and fall of Professor Stevens's fluid voice. The words were so far removed from modern English it sounded like a romantic foreign language. The poetry flowed from the esteemed woman's shapely lips, melting over Chelsea's already wet skin. She lost herself in the hypnotic quality of the rhyme and meter, no longer thinking of Chaucer and tricky transla-tions but of far more sensual matters.

Snapping back into reality, she realized that the steady cadence of Professor Stevens's recitation had been replaced by the crisp annunciation of her name. The nervous stares of her peers bore into her back as Chelsea realized she was being called on. She knew none of the other students envied her. It wasn't a good thing to be singled out in one of Professor Stevens's lectures. She felt her face grow hot and red as she lifted her gaze to meet the professor's critical stare.

"You are not going to make me repeat myself, are you, Chelsea?"

"Wha—? Um...no..." A pitiful stutter of syllables was all she could manage with the weight of Professor Stevens's obvious disapproval bearing down on her.

"Come to the front of the room, please." The professor's precise articulation resounded deep within Chelsea's core. There was something about the way Professor Stevens formed her words that was beyond intriguing. Sometimes she would get so lost in the depths of her silky voice she would miss the words the professor was actually saying.

Peeling her soft, sun-kissed skin off the chair, Chelsea tentatively looked from left to right trying to see which direction would be easiest to traverse. The seat she had chosen was right smack in the middle of the long rows of gradually inclining desks. A line of students occupied the desks on either side of her, leaving no easy exit. As she tried to scoot past the endless row of seated legs, down the narrow backpack-laden path, she heard the sound of Professor Stevens's boots tapping along the tile floor. Pausing, Chelsea turned toward the front of the lecture hall.

"What are you doing? It is going to take you the whole class period to get down here that way. Come down the front. And don't step on anyone," Professor Stevens commanded, her voice never rising above its usual smooth, calm tone.

Chelsea glanced down the sloping stadium seating before her. The route was anything but clear; more than half the desks on the way down to the lecture floor were filled. She took a deep breath and gracelessly climbed over the empty chair directly in front of her. Her dress hiked up revealing long, lean legs as she stepped onto the empty seat. One row down, three more to go.

The next line of desks was occupied by a group of young jocks. Forced to go through the middle of them, she braced herself against the plastic backs of the next row of chairs. Aiming for the narrow space between the broad shoulders of two blond-haired powerhouses, she lifted her left leg up and snaked it between them. Momentarily off balance, Chelsea felt a rough hand creep beneath her spread-wide dress and firmly grasp her round ass. A startled gasp burst from her lips at the intrusion. She quickly moved to bring her right leg over the row of connected chairs and get away from the hand currently groping her.

"I don't recall asking for your help, David. Please remove your hand and let her do it on her own," Professor Stevens's voice rang out over the palpable silence in the lecture hall. The hand firmly clutching Chelsea's buttocks quickly loosened and fell from beneath her skirt. When Professor Stevens asked you to do something, you did it. She took in a relieved breath, hoping David hadn't been able to notice just how wet she was, and made quick work descending the next two rows. Unsure if it was from the rush of adrenaline or just her getting inappropriately turned on, she knew her panties were growing increasingly damp.

Staggering over the last row of chairs, Chelsea finally made it to the lecture-hall floor. Nervously smoothing the short cotton skirt of her dress, she stopped before the tall, voluptuous figure of Professor Stevens. A sleek black pencil skirt hugged her generous curves while a deep purple button-down accentuated the professor's narrow waist. Chelsea couldn't tear her eyes away from the woman staring down at her.

"What do you have to say for yourself? I'd like to hear what possible reason you have for not paying attention while I am talking." Her liquid voice washed over Chelsea's skin, sending a wave of nerves and heat down her spine.

"I—I'm sorry," Chelsea replied in a low whisper. She lowered her face, too ashamed to meet the professor's eyes.

The cool, firm pressure of fingertips grabbing her by the chin forced her to raise her gaze. Professor Stevens's hard green eyes bore into her flushed face. With a quick tug, the professor forced Chelsea's mouth open. Her arms hanging uselessly by her sides, she didn't struggle against the maneuver. The only indication that she was far from comfortable with the contact was the ever-deepening reddish hue of her cheeks.

Holding Chelsea's delicate face tilted back at a severe angle, Professor Stevens leaned down and inhaled deeply.

"Is that booze on your breath?" she asked, roughly tossing Chelsea's face away in disgust. "Your disrespect is nauseating. Do you need a lesson in how to treat your betters? Do you need me to remind you of your place in this classroom?"

Chelsea knew it was a rhetorical question. There was no point in replying, she was going to get a lesson and deep down she knew she deserved it. She lowered her eyes to the worn linoleum floor and awaited her instructions.

"Give me your dress," Professor Stevens commanded in a low voice.

Chelsea gaped at the woman standing before her. She wanted her to strip down to her underwear in front of a lecture hall full of people? Embarrassment, disbelief and a creeping excitement washed over her.

"I'll not repeat myself. You will do as you are told. Now hand me your dress." Chelsea couldn't disobey the fierce finality of the professor's tone. With a shaky sigh, she lifted the thin white cotton dress over her head and tentatively placed the sweat-dampened wad of fabric in the professor's waiting hand.

Wearing only a pale-pink bra and matching panties, Chelsea awkwardly stood with every eye in the room upon her. She shifted her weight, first to her left foot then to her right, unable to stand still before her classmates. She didn't have very long to dwell on her exposure before Professor Stevens gave her something else to think about.

While Chelsea had been floundering in her discomfort, the tall and busty Professor Stevens sauntered behind the long wooden desk at the front of the hall. From beneath the rickety podium, she pulled out the leather-bound briefcase she carried with her to every lecture she gave. The cotton dress grasped in one hand, she used the other to pop the metal hinges on the case leaving the lid ominously open and angled in such a way as to obscure its contents from curious eyes.

The brisk movement of white fabric filling the air caught Chelsea's attention. The professor's perfectly manicured hands carefully folded the wrinkled dress before placing it in the briefcase. A new wave of perspiration having nothing to do with the temperature of the room erupted over Chelsea's body. Was she going to get her dress back? How was she supposed to get to her next class? Or get home?

Out from the depths of the dark, foreboding case, Professor Stevens pulled a bright red apple. Chelsea couldn't help but notice the way the crisp crimson contrasted exquisitely against the porcelain skin of her instructor's hand. With delicate reverence, she brought the fruit up to her mouth. Instead of biting into the taut skin, the professor merely inhaled deeply. Clearly pleased by its sweet, ripe scent, she allowed her full, rosy lips to slowly spread into a faint smile.

Any warmth behind the subtle upturn of her lips was quickly extinguished by the cold stare she gave Chelsea the moment her dark eyelashes shot up. Boots clicking on the hard surface of the floor, Professor Stevens took her time walking back around to the front of the desk, to where Chelsea's exposed, golden flesh waited.

"Since you clearly do not have anything to say for yourself, I don't see any need for you to be able to use your mouth."

Firmly gripping her face once again, Professor Stevens forced the girl's mouth open before the thought of protesting could even cross her mind. Hand still locked on her jaw, she popped the Red Delicious between Chelsea's glossed lips.

"Now don't even think of letting that apple fall. I will be forced to take disciplinary action if you do," she said, her voice flowing like liquid silk. Giving her chin a demeaning little shake, she released Chelsea's flushed face.

Though she tried to avoid it, Chelsea could feel her sharp teeth penetrate the smooth, firm skin of the apple. She cringed the moment the sweet juice leaked into her mouth. A cruel smile lighted Professor Stevens's face as she watched her struggle not to let her jaw give in and bite into the ripe red orb. The heat of Chelsea's humiliation radiated from her skin, filling her with the knowledge that her face was now the same bright shade of red as the fruit wedged between her lips.

The sharp tug on the knot of blonde hair on the back of her head nearly pulled her off balance. Chelsea tried not to cry out at the piercing pain spreading across her scalp as Professor Stevens dragged her by the hair as if it were a leash and she were a disobedient puppy. Her legs struggled to keep up as she was led by the ponytail across the front of the lecture hall.

The apple nearly flew from her lips as the professor walked her right up to the edge of the long wooden desk. With a deep thud, Chelsea's body was forced over the top. She knew there was going to be a long bruise along her hips from the impact. A wave of shame and agony flooded her. She wasn't sure what made her more uncomfortable, the room full of people watching her be humiliated or the growing heat swirling between her legs.

Without a word Professor Stevens let go of her blonde locks and moved her hands down the length of Chelsea's exposed back. With a rough jerk, the professor tugged her sweat- and lust-drenched panties off her ass, letting them fall about her ankles.

"These are soaked through. This is turning you on, isn't it? You are clearly enjoying this too much for it to be teaching you anything. I'll just have to fix that."

Click, click, click. The slow echo of the professor's boots as she walked down the length of the desk sent a terrifying and thrilling chill down Chelsea's spine. The sound was quickly replaced by a loud, solid smack. A harsh moan crept out of her mouth and slipped around the slick skin of the apple. Tendrils of white-hot pain spread across the flesh of her bare ass. Before she had a chance to catch her breath Professor Stevens brought the next swing of the heavy, red-bound copy of *The Collected Works of Chaucer* down upon her buttocks.

The explosion of pain was more than she could bear. Chelsea's teeth sank farther into the juicy apple, prying her jaw apart. The round fruit made it so she couldn't swallow, but the sweet juice bursting from the tight red skin into her mouth made her salivate nearly uncontrollably. Tears, juice and spit dripped down her face, smearing her makeup to form a sticky puddle on the desktop.

The strikes came harder and harder. Screams erupted in muffled desperation from behind the sweet red ball. Chelsea's futile attempts to kick and step away only resulted in harder spanks and a tangled mess of feet and panties. Just when she didn't think her tender ass could take any more, that the prickles of heat and agony were more than she could handle, she was bombarded with a whole different kind of pain.

The professor yanked her hips so that she was still bent over the desk, but now there were a few inches of space between the wood and her thighs. Chelsea could hear the delicate fabric of her panties tear as she was forced to spread her legs farther apart with a swift kick from her professor's booted foot. With another sharp crack her entire body blossomed in exquisite pain. Professor Stevens had changed tactics and now brought the power of her bare hand across Chelsea's swollen, dripping cunt.

She repeated the sharp upward strike directly on her aching lips and electrified nerves. "You are nothing," the professor articulated, punctuating each statement with another fierce slap right on her pussy. "Inconsequential. Rude. Dirty. Depraved. Trash."

Pausing momentarily, Professor Stevens gripped Chelsea's sweaty blonde hair and pulled her head off the desk. "You are going to come in front of this whole room of people. You are going to come from the sheer ecstasy of my giving you a lesson. You are going to show me the respect I deserve by coming at the severity of my hand."

Chelsea's head fell into the sea of salty-sweet spittle covering the desk when the professor roughly dropped her hair. Her whole body trembled with shame, need, desire and the will to please the professor.

Falling quickly back into a staccato rhythm of loud, hard, spanks on her throbbing cunt, Professor Stevens demanded her orgasm. She didn't have to wait long. A rush of thick, hot pleasure melded with the sharp pain and sent Chelsea into a body-thrashing climax. She hung limply over the edge of the desk, apple in mouth, hair and face covered in her own drool, thighs wet with her come. It was only when the smooth sound of Professor Stevens's liquid voice edged in on her postorgasmic haze that she began to stir.

"You are not going to make me repeat myself, are you, Chelsea?" She forced her eyes open, anxious to see what else the professor had in store for her.

Wiping the little droplet of spittle from her chin, she glanced around in confusion only to see the nervous faces of her classmates. The room was still sweltering and her stomach still reeled with the discomfort of a hangover, but she was fully clothed and back in the middle of the stadium style seats.

"Umm...I'm sorry Professor Stevens," she replied quietly. She could feel her face redden at the thought of how this had played out in her mind only moments before.

"See me after class. We need to discuss your lack of respect and find a suitable solution."

REPENT!
OR, GOD
NEVER SAW
ME COMING

David Wraith

I couldn't help but wonder what it would feel like to be spanked by a woman who believed in God. Being a lapsed Catholic, I figured I could guess how a Catholic woman would go about it. She'd probably light candles and burn incense first. She'd be sensual about it. She wouldn't hit too hard for fear that taking too much pleasure in someone else's pain would be a sin.

A Baptist would do it to a rhythm. Like the fast hand clap of a gospel song. She might even beat my ass with a tambourine.

I think a hard-core fundamentalist would be the best. There was this woman who used to stand outside the abortion clinic where I used to volunteer, shouting into a megaphone, calling us baby killers and murderers. I bet she'd love to take me across her knee and light up my ass with a wooden paddle, all full of righteous indignation and religious fervor. She'd probably start speaking in tongues.

Not counting the nuns in grammar school, I'd never been spanked by a true believer. Sonia, my girlfriend, was an atheist.

She was the most beautiful atheist I'd ever seen.

One of the occupational hazards of being a sexual deviant is that people ask you innocent questions that you cannot honestly or completely answer. People would see me and Sonia, two attractive, educated, urbane twentysomethings together, smile approvingly and ask, "So how did you two meet?" Well, it's a funny story...

It was my senior year in college and I was taking a performance art class, because that's what you did your senior year in college. The class had no textbook and no written homework. In lieu of a final exam, the students had to appear in a performance art festival at a local gallery. My piece was this Max Ernst meets Yoko Ono thing where I sat wearing only a G-string and a blindfold before a black leather bench covered with whips, floggers, bondage tape and other tools, inviting anyone who cared to, to use them on me as they saw fit.

After two hours of my being poked, prodded and tentatively whacked by amateurs, art aficionados and the odd, closeted academic sadist, in walked Sonia. Her soft hands caressed my face for a moment before she removed my blindfold and I was staring at this beautiful amazon with pale white skin, dyed red hair and ice-blue colored contact lenses, her face vaguely reminiscent of an American flag. She drew her hands across my body and I noticed her impeccable mismatched manicures: long, blood-red nails on her left hand and short nails with clear polish on her right. She would later explain that her left hand was for the boys and her right hand was for the ladies. She was bisexual *and* ambidextrous.

She instructed me to stand and turned me around to face the wall. She selected a roll of plastic wrap from the bench and quickly encased me from neck to knees. She lit a candle from the bench and circled me, holding it in her hand, flicking wax on my back as it melted. We fell into a rhythm where I could anticipate the singes that were dulled only slightly by the thin plastic barrier. The confidence and efficiency of her movements were hypnotic. Behind me I could hear the nearby chatter dying down as people stopped talking to watch Sonia work. Once my back was thoroughly covered in wax, she stood between me and the bench, looking at me over her shoulder while she blew out the candle. She took a pair of scissors from the bench and cut through the plastic wrap along my shoulders and back. The plastic that was weighed down by the wax fell away, leaving the front of my body encased, but my back, my ass and the backs of my thighs exposed. She took my riding crop and held it in her short-nailed hand, circling me and swinging it back and forth in front of her.

She lightly tapped me with the riding crop, covering my entire backside with soft blows before increasing the intensity. Her timing was like a metronome. It was like she was applying separate coats of paint to my skin. By the fifth pass, my body was vibrating like a tuning fork being softly struck to produce a low-frequency hum.

She stopped suddenly. I returned to my senses. It was like coming out of a swimming pool and having the water drain from my ears. She stood in front of me, smiled and ripped the remaining plastic wrap from my body in one swift tug and I came harder than I'd ever come without having sex. I was so startled, ejaculating in the middle of a downtown art gallery, that I felt dizzy for a moment and forgot where I was. She kissed me and tucked her calling card into my jockstrap.

So when people ask how we met, we just smile and say that we met at an art gallery.

I was an English major at Sonia's safety school. She was a chemical engineering major at the school I applied to and didn't get accepted by. In addition to her scholarship and work-study program, Sonia was occasionally in the employ of a dominatrix named Mistress Monika.

Mistress Monika was a Satanist. She was the most beautiful Satanist I'd ever seen. She was tall, blonde and imposing. Together, she and Sonia looked like a panel from a *Wonder Woman* comic book.

Mistress Monika held parties that were the stuff of urban legend. They were invitation only, and the invitation came with a liability waiver and nondisclosure agreement.

When I arrived to pick Sonia up for one such party, she answered the door in a black, see-through mesh dress with anatomically guestimated strips of vinyl to make it street legal. I was wearing a black suit and black button-down shirt and a black collar with a metal ring.

The party was packed, mostly with couples. Naked submissives worked the room serving drinks.

The guests moved to the basement where the Mistress kept her various apparatuses of torture; if I'm not mistaken, it was also where her legion of Haitian zombies hid during daylight hours.

An overweight, balding man in a leather vest and assless chaps had a girl in a Catholic school uniform bent over a wooden horse and was paddling her. Sonia caught me looking at them, slipped a finger through the metal ring of my collar, pulled my face toward hers and commanded, "Strip."

I walked to the back corner of the room and folded my clothes over a chair. The soles of my bare feet on the cold cement floor made me shiver, but I was sure that a good sound thrashing would warm me up.

I joined Sonia at her side. She took me by the collar and led me to a spot near the wall where a pair of leather wrist restraints was suspended from beams in the unfinished ceiling. I rested my arms in the restraints while she chose from a selection of the homemade canes she carried in her tool bag.

No matter how many beatings I'd taken, I was always nervous. I never knew exactly how my body and mind would process the pain. Sometimes it was a meditative, almost spiritual experience. I'd lose time, and the harshest blows simply tickled as I felt that I was leaving my body. Sometimes it was intensely erotic. Each strike seemed to be landing on some meridian that connected directly to my dick.

And sometimes...it just fucking hurt.

I was afraid that this would be one of those times. I should have been excited, but instead I was running through a mental checklist of everything I'd eaten that day. Had I had enough protein? Had I had enough carbs? Or was she about to beat me into a hypoglycemic seizure...again.

I never told Sonia about this nervousness, but I didn't have to. I'm quite sure she could tell. Half of what she knew about me came from the things I told her, the other half came from things she observed while beating me up. That's why she liked to prolong the moment before the first blow landed for as long as possible: just to fuck with my head.

She stood in front of me tossing the cane in the air and catching it, hefting it for weight, bending it slightly to see how much it gave. She swiped at the air a couple of times, making swashbuckling noises, like in an old Errol Flynn movie. She ground the rounded tip of the cane into the center of my chest and I closed my eyes and took a deep breath as she traced it across my nipple.

She stepped behind me and traced the tip of the cane along my spine. I exhaled a sigh, rolled my hips in anticipation and rocked onto the balls of my feet with nervous energy. I could almost hear the smile spreading across Sonia's face. This is what she called "giving it up," when my body told on me. I try to act like I don't want it when I do. I try to act like it doesn't hurt when it does. This façade was an affront to Sonia's professional vanity and her goal was always to shatter it. I don't want to give it up, but I do.

She knew I was ready. Soon she would hit me and everything would be all better. Or worse. But, at least I would know. I heard the cane slice through the air and land smack dab across my ass. My whole body tensed for a split second and then everything released. My arms went slack against the wrist restraints. My clenched fists turned into splayed fingers. My head dropped and rolled across my shoulders. She built a strong steady rhythm; all wrist and forearm. She was just getting warmed up. I was just getting used to the delicious stripes she was putting across my ass when the music suddenly changed.

Now, the music at these events almost always sucked: Pseudo–New Age Pop shit. Midwestern sexual deviants over forty all seem to think that the sun rises on Enya and sets on Enigma. Personally, I saw nothing sexy about the chants of Gregorian monks or watching someone get whipped to *Sadness Part 1* for the thousandth time. This night however, Sonia had put together the playlist. The song "Heroin" started to play. "Heroin," 1966, recorded by the Velvet Underground, composed by Lou Reed: seven minutes twelve seconds.

The caning abruptly stopped. I almost jumped out of my skin when Sonia grabbed me from behind, pressed herself into my back and whispered in my ear, "You. Are. So. Fucked."

She put down the cane and came back with a flogger in each hand. Sonia was surgical with a flogger. She could make it feel like being teased with a feather duster or being smacked with a phone book by the secret police of an Eastern Bloc nation.

Now she had two floggers and was beating me, Florentine style, to the Velvet Underground. It was like getting smacked with two phone books. Repeatedly. In 4/4 time. Or like accidentally backing into a windmill.

She swung both arms back and forth, rolling one wrist off the other and forming a relentless barrage of leather. One flogger was barely off my body before the next one landed.

Seven minutes and twelve seconds later, I was spent. I was pulling the restraints as far as they would go, throwing my hips forward and walking in place as if I could get away. At this point I was willing to tell her anything: where the slaves were hiding, that I had Jews in my basement, who was a communist, who stole the Glengarry leads, anything just to make her stop.

"Where do you think you're going?" She wrapped her arm around me. It was slick with sweat, as was my entire body. She teased my cock with the straps of the flogger in her left hand and then gave me one good whack across my ass with the one in her right. She pressed her body to mine. We were both so sweaty that we were sliding off each other. Feeling her bare breasts and erect nipples against my back, it was only then that I realized she was naked. Somewhere between putting down the cane and picking up the floggers, she'd slipped out of her dress.

My eyes darted to the faces in the crowd, most of whom had stopped what they were doing to watch us. I'd been so deep in my own headspace that I hadn't noticed how Sonia's nudity had been betrayed by the expressions on the other guests' faces. The people gathered in this room represented hundreds of years of sexual depravity between them. They'd done things most people would never even read about, but to look at them you'd think they'd never seen a handsome, naked, English student get the daylights beaten out of him by a sexy, naked, chemical engineer.

Sonia cut me down. "Go get me a chair," she said.

She sat down, grabbed my arm and jerked me over her knee. She traced her finger along my spine and lovingly caressed my ass, which must have felt like Braille with all the rod-sized wets she'd raised on it.

She started spanking me. There's a certain detachment to beating someone with a whip or a cane, even for Sonia for whom these tools were like extensions of her own body. But when it's skin to skin, there's a carnal sensation that was even too much for Sonia and her normal icy demeanor. There was something frenzied about the way she was spanking my ass with her bare hand. Her normal control was gone. I could feel it in the way her belly expanded and contracted against my hip as her breathing became labored. She wasn't pacing herself. She wasn't saving anything for later. She wanted this as much as I did. More. For once, it was Sonia who was "giving it up." If I didn't know better, I would have thought she'd just received the Holy Spirit.

My cock grew hard against her lap, and I was grinding it into the soft flesh of her thighs to take my mind off the pain she was inflicting. She caught me with a good one out of nowhere. White-hot pain shot through my ass, right up my spine. I turned my head to see her vigorously trying to shake the sting out of her spanking hand. Our eyes met and she just shoved me off of her with both hands.

My world was upended for a moment. I shook my head to regain my bearings. At first, all I saw were the beams of Mistress Monika's unfinished ceiling, then a naked amazon stepping over me, lowering herself onto my throbbing erection.

The heel of her hand was pressed against my sternum while she angrily thrust her hips into mine, grinding her ass into my thighs. That's when I saw it. I threw my head back and there it was. On the back wall, right between Assless Chaps Man and Catholic School Girl, there was a black and red tapestry: an inverted pentagram with a goat's head inside. A Satanic symbol.

Then it hit me. This good Catholic boy was naked in a room full of strangers in the basement of a Satanist being fucked blind by a woman who did not believe that she nor I had an immortal soul. Just as I was about to come I reached up and grabbed Sonia's head with both hands and yelled, "GET THEE BEHIND ME, SATAN!"

Staring upside down at the pentagram tapestry as my body shuddered and convulsed, I exploded inside of her with one thought running through my mind: I had to go to church. I had to run to church. Not out of religious obligation, but because I needed Jesus!

Fast-forward ten years. Sonia and I are no longer together. I'm dating a Quaker. The most beautiful Quaker I've ever seen. I run a Catholic prayer group. Now, there are some occupational hazards to being a sexual deviant *and* running a Catholic prayer group. Parishioners sometimes ask innocent questions that I cannot honestly or completely answer. When someone asks about my faith journey, I don't tell him it all started one night when I was hanging naked from the ceiling of a Satanist's basement getting my ass beaten with a cane. I just smile and say, "Well, I guess I was able to find God because God never saw me coming."

BELOW STAIRS

T. R. Verten

This is only the fifth time Hannah had been over to play with them, but she and Cassie hit it off almost immediately. Their chemistry was off the charts, he could tell, and after the second session his wife would not stop talking about her. It seemed like every other sentence was "Hannah this…" or "Hannah that…" and he could tell that it got her hot because she would bring the other woman up without fail, even when he was eating her out.

"God, baby," she'd drawl, "those knee-highs just kill me, you know? Having her all spread out over my knee, naked from the waist down, and oh"—her voice going up an octave in time with his tongue, and she breathed out—"fuck that's nice. Right there, such a good boy. You know how I like it."

They'd been chatting, too, online, Cas tapping away on her side of the bed, occasionally letting out interested noises, a breathy *hello* or *okay then*. So when she did come over, again, it was at Cassie's behest. "I like her," she told him point blank when they were out on their weekly Friday date—Indian, probably not the best choice for sex and romance, but Boston is cold in January; it requires the heat of warming spices to take the edge off.

"Should we email her?" he said, and she interrupted, "Oh, I'll take care of that," in a way that made him think she had already broached the subject without telling him first.

Hannah takes a taxi there; her cheeks are a high pink when Cassie opens the door.

"Hi!" she says, stepping inside, and they all exchange cheek-to-cheek kisses. "Honey," Cassie says, looking pointedly at the overnight bag, "don't be rude."

"Of course," Patrick says, "May I take that for you?"

"Oh, gosh, thanks!"

"Let's go on through," Cas says, "I've got a nice Sancerre open." She steers Hannah into the living room, and Patrick goes the other way, into the guest bedroom. He places the bag—black with brown handles—at the foot of the bed, before returning to the two women. They are sipping wine; a third glass, already poured, waits for him on the coffee table. The women chat next to each other on the couch and he watches—Cassie offering Hannah a refill, their fingers touching lightly as she steadies the stem—and listens.

"We went to Saint Lucia, god, ages ago, wasn't it?"

"Winter of two-thousand-five," he says.

"Did you like it?"

"Everything except the sunburn," Cas laughs.

"And," he adds, "the mosquitoes."

Hannah tucks her legs underneath her. "I never get bitten."

"Oh, lucky you!" Cassie says. "Patrick tried to take me camping once and I had to go and sleep in the car, that's how chewed up I was."

"It was bad," he admits.

"Poor you," says Hannah, setting her glass down.

"Indeed. Curse of the redheads or something." Cassie answers, and then leaning into Hannah's cardigan-sweatered shoulder, adds, "I'd bite you."

Hannah snorts, because the line is cheesy, but she receives the kiss that follows easily enough. "Mmm," she says, her mouth smushing slightly when Cassie reaches across her body to set down her own wineglass. They have been here before, with other girls at other times, and Patrick is more than happy to watch his wife fondle the pert, perfect breasts of a twenty-five-year-old, and he may get hard, but this interval between the front door and the basement is not about his cock but his wife's wetness, Hannah's willingness. When they're alone, his cock usually has to wait a punishingly long time for physical satisfaction. When they've got a girl over, and he's not the focus, Patrick can count on not only getting off sooner, but getting off more lightly, in every sense of the word.

When the two women break for air, Patrick has polished off the wine, but it is Hannah's cheeks that are flushed. She stands up, demure even though her white blouse is unbuttoned past her bra, and says that she needs the toilet before they get started. "Guest bathroom," Cassie says, "and your bag is in there." She points toward the guest bedroom.

"Great, back in a bit," she tells them.

"Do you want to go on down?" Cassie asks, standing to gather the glasses.

"Can do," he says. At the top of the stairs he turns the basement lights on, where most of the scene is set up already. He uses the half bath—half-hard, it takes a few moments for him to go—and washes his hands thoroughly, drying them on a faded rust-red towel, once vibrant, now relegated to the basement.

Hannah's robe is pale blue like her eyes; Cassie's is black. He meets them at the base of the stairs: Cassie automatically dims the lights, and says, "Much better."

This time, when they sit on the couch, Cassie settles in next to him, and in an anxious throaty voice says, "Take it off for us, pretty baby." Hannah looks around shyly, like there might be someone else in the room. When she undoes the satin belt Cassie coos, and when she opens her robe they exchange a heated look. "God," she says, as Cassie moves her hand to his thigh, "you are so fucking hot."

"She really is," he says. His wife is stroking along his fly, holding out her other hand to the girl. "Come here, you beautiful little bitch," and Hannah steps over the pile of discarded silk cautiously, before coming to sit on Patrick's lap as instructed and meeting his lips in a kiss Cassie pushes her in for. As they make out, tongues touching and drawing back in curt flicks, her cunt growing damp against his thigh, her underwear is yanked down, her bra strap slides down her shoulder. Cassie breathes hot words of encouragement, growing bolder, touching herself and him and her and them, all three of them.

"I want to see this little slut on her knees, don't you?" she asks him. "Look at her, humping your leg like a filthy animal. She can barely contain herself," and it is true, Hannah is sliding up and down his quadriceps, and he has to place his hands around her slim waist to hold her still, and even then she whimpers, pathetically.

"Oh sweetheart," Cassie says, pushing the girl's dark hair away from her wide blue eyes, "you have so much farther to go. Come on, get down," she insists, and when Hannah does not listen right away Cassie fists a hand in her hair and pulls her down onto the floor. "I said get the fuck *down* you dirty bitch. Get on your fucking knees. Who the fuck do you think you are?" The soles of her shoes are scuffed—this is the detail he notices as she crawls behind Cas to the joist. Her slit is already damp, her ass perfectly round. It jiggles as she crawls.

"Sit up; that's a good girl," his wife says, stripping down to her own ensemble. The black silk and lace is vibrant against her white skin. The flame of her hair matches the redness of Hannah's nipples as Cassie pinches them. "Keep those hands up," she says, slapping her tits until those go pink as well.

Cas has had some rope training. Hannah sits as instructed, knees splayed out wide, buttocks resting on her stripper heels as her hair is parted and tied to the joist. The two pigtails his wife ties make Hannah look like a schoolgirl, hands bound behind her neck so that her young breasts beg to be suckled and smacked. With a loud sound Cassie winches the wood up high so that Hannah is pulled up by her hair.

"Come touch her," she tells him, because he is looking on, hungrily. The permission is so much quicker than with just the two of them, because now Hannah is the focus. "Help me play with these nice tits." He stands up, his cock stiff, his gaze aimed steadily down at the shivering, naked girl trussed up like a piece of meat, and walks in a slow, appraising circle around her, taking in the hold-up stockings, the bra yanked cruelly down around her rib cage, the pale-brown rope cleaving her hairline in two.

In their emails to one another Cassie must have inquired about the sensitivity of Hannah's nipples, because she pulls and prods and pinches one, and with soft clucks encourages him to do the same. When Hannah's tits are burning pink from play, Cassie clamps them. The chain between them swings as Cassie stands Patrick up and undoes his belt, "Hold her hair, honey," she tells him, "Grab those pigtails and fuck her face. Stupid little slut, that mouth is begging for a cock."

Hannah opens her mouth obediently, like a baby bird, and Cassie guides his swollen cockhead to the center of her moist lower lip and swipes off the precome gathering there. She presents the girl with this offering and says, "Lick it off," and Hannah does, hungrily. Cassie says, "You want to suck on this cock, baby?" and she says, "Yes, yes, please." She twists against her restraints, seeking friction, seeking relief.

"Please, what?" Cassie says, taunting her with his dick, both of them her toys.

"Please, Mistress, let me suck him off."

"That's a good girl," she says, patting Hannah's head as she closes her eyes and starts to suck. "Eyes up here," she says, walking behind Patrick and tugging out his balls for the girl to lick and draw into her mouth, one at a time. "Keep those eyes open while you suck that dick. Aren't you a good girl? How's that feel, baby?" she asks him.

"Christ," he says, sawing his hips back and forth between her spit-slick lips. "So fucking good. Thank you."

"Deep throat him," she tells the girl, her voice rich with amusement. She grips one rope in each hand to pull her by the hair, and he says, "Oh, fuck yes." She purrs, "Suck it, whore, there you go, choke on that fat cock. You want to make him come for me? Can you do that, can you get a load on that pretty face of yours?"

Hannah nods, makes a garbled, wet sound around his dick, and Cassie releases one rope and says, "What's that?" and Hannah doesn't even answer, she dives right back down, forging down hot and purposeful on his throbbing dick. "You want that come, huh? Yeah, earn it," she says. Another choked nod is her answer, and Hannah gags around his cock, hollowing her cheeks and swallowing over and over until he says, "Baby, babe, I'm gonna—" and she practically shouts, "Pull out, pull out," and he starts to come in her throat and finishes with Cassie's hand wrapped around his own, milking his load across the girl's pretty face.

"Fuck," he groans, his heart pounding in his ears, taking in the sight of her—eye makeup streaked, hair straining at the ropes, come dripping down her cheek—and his dick twitches even after he tucks himself away at the sight of Cassie pulling down her underwear and straddling Hannah's eager upturned face.

"My turn."

He watches from the side, listening to the crescendo of her first orgasm and then—after an interval where she plays with the clamps, opening and closing them so that they pinch and Hannah squeaks, and Cassie smacks her tits, slaps her face, shoves her fingers down Hannah's throat and then dips them down between her legs to fondle her as she whispers in her ear, dark quiet things that make Hannah whimper, *"Please, oh, please"*—a second orgasm, where she rides her, hands grabbing the ropes like reins and her own hips bucking with release.

She dismounts and takes a step back to survey her work, to touch her again. Those big blue eyes widen in surprise when Cassie pauses in her caresses to slap Hannah across the face, in between slaps prodding and pressing her cheeks so that her lips pooch out.

"Baby," she says, in that wet scratchy voice that gets him in his gut, "I think it's time for this girl to get fucked, what do you think?"

"Fantastic idea," he says, "Do you need the bag?"

"Please," she says, drawing circles on Hannah's abdomen with her dark nails. She lifts her arms gingerly, and he straps her into the harness, buckling it in the back around her ample hips.

"I'll need a condom," she says, and he retrieves one of those as well, unlubricated. "Hey," she breathes out as he tears open the packet, "baby, come on, come get me wet before you put that on." Patrick grins and touches his lips gingerly to the tip of the cock, licks a slow circle either way and, when she tuts, he draws it in slowly between his teeth. She hisses, "Be glad that's not real, sweetheart, you could hurt someone with those things."

He slips the condom on her, and she positions herself behind Hannah, pushing up from underneath until the girl is suspended over the cock, the head just teasing the entrance to her cunt, and she sobs with frustration because there is no more slack with her hair, no way for her to reach it.

"Beg me for it."

"Oh, god, please, please, I want it, anything," the girl babbles to the air, the basement walls, to anyone who will listen.

"What do you think?" she asks Patrick, not that his answer matters.

"Give her a treat," he says, and she purrs, "Isn't that nice of him, sweetheart? He's so much nicer than me. Okay, here you go, let's fill that tight hole of yours." Cassie cups the girl's breasts and sits up on her own heels, pushing inside—he can tell by the harsh cry of relief Hannah emits.

"Go to the front," she tells him, after an interval of teasing and slow fucking. "I want you to put your mouth on her." He crawls around to the front and catches her gaze: bleary-eyed and desperate. On all fours he licks her as Cas fucks her, occasionally catching the slick of silicone and latex on his tongue. From above him he hears her keeping up the same crescendo of "Good girl," "Slut," "So hot."

Twice Hannah's hips go fast like she may be on the verge of coming, and when she seems close Cassie stills her own hips and commands him to stop. After the third time she says, voice broken, "Get the wand." She covers Hannah's mouth, her teeth visible in a rictus of pleasure-pain; fucks her hard against the vibrations, and when the girl finally comes it is with tears that leave her eyeliner tracking in wet lines down her face.

"Fu—uck," she moans as they pull the orgasm from her: it sounds feral, hardly pleasurable. Her body tenses, twitches. Cassie backs off and says, "Turn it up," and the girl grits her teeth and spasms between them, each small cry like a miniature climax, and when it happens again only the pressure of Cassie's hand keeps the sound down.

"Yes, that's it, there you go, baby, there you go," Cas intones, gentling her through it.

Of course she is shaking, vibrating with aftershocks. They each unhook a pigtail, quickly, and Cas unties her hands and rubs her wrists. Patrick takes away all the toys—Hannah hisses when he unhooks the clamps—and puts them into the half bath to deal with later, bringing back three bottles of water from the minifridge and handing one to each of the girls, who are by now curled up under a ratty yellow duvet on the couch.

"Mmm, thank you," says Hannah. He smiles around the mouth of his own bottle and gets out his phone to make a call. Cas strokes Hannah's hair intermittently, a small smile playing on her lips. The girls look content, comfortable, like they've been doing this for years, rather than a couple of months, and when the doorbell chimes, signaling their dinner has arrived, he knows it is nowhere near the last time.

IN THE CHILL OF HER DISPLEASURE

Veronica Wilde

The spring twilight is just beginning to cool when the dommes and slaves arrive for Carima's salon. One by one they park in the circular drive and ring the bell: five women in Christian Louboutins and Jimmy Choos, formidable from their blood-red manicures to their confident eyes. And behind them, six boys, whose expressions range from intimidated to excited.

Carima's slave, Liam, has already built the fire and has been waiting in the foyer. "They're here."

She caresses his tousled blond hair. "Then let them in."

He squares his shoulders. The tension in his jaw amuses her. Liam is young; she is his first mistress. He's been her slave ever since they met at a fetish ball seven months ago, arriving every weekend to run her bath, wash her car and clean her stable. She keeps him naked whenever possible, hard cock on display, so she can use him at a moment's notice, his pretty mouth gagged and his dick buried deep inside her. Already he serves beautifully, can take the hardest spanking and obeys perfectly whether he's cuffed or leashed or caged. Yet preparing for this salon has had him on edge all day.

Liam opens the carved oak door, playing butler with equal nervousness and courtesy. The dommes give him admiring looks as they file into the polished parquet foyer. Of the six boys following behind them, two are accompanying their mistresses and the other four are uncollared. They are here as an audition of sorts; tonight is the first in what is to be a monthly femdom salon and it is the slaves' job to serve drinks and refreshments, give foot rubs and tend the fire. If these boys perform well, they may find a mistress here.

"Let's go into the living room." Carima runs a critical eye over the new boys. They're a good-looking lot, athletic and long limbed. The tallest one is dark haired and handsome, and gives her a look of brazen sexual assessment as he passes. Well, then. Someone has a lesson in subservience to learn.

The boys undress in the adjoining dungeon, then return, kneel and give their names. The handsome, cocky one is Colton, who kneels with the dignity of a captured soldier. Every slave in the room is sporting a stiff cock and the tension of their flexed thigh muscles is exquisite. But all eyes are on Colton and his little smirk says he knows it: every domme in the room is eyeing his thick, enormous cock.

Carima notices that Liam is watching Colton, albeit with a scowl. If she didn't know better, she'd think he was jealous. She prods him. "Take the boys into the kitchen to begin serving."

He nods, suddenly looking so vulnerable and buff at the same time that it gives her a protective pang in her chest.

"At last," Carima says, settling back into her chaise. The warmth of the flames intensifies the light scent of daffodils and irises around the room. "I'm glad we started these salons. It's so hard to find time to see each other these days."

"It's good training for them as well," throws in the oldest domme, Anne.

"Training, schmaining," Stephanie scoffs. "I just want to relax. How is Irving, Carima? You haven't mentioned any competitions lately."

The newest domme turns. "You enter your slave in competitions?"

The rest of them erupt into laughter, though Carima enjoys the fleeting image of an equestrian competition for submissive men. "Irving is my horse. My slave is named Liam," she corrects.

Predictable jokes about bits and riding crops ensue as the naked slaves return with the trays of refreshments. They are being judged on their manners and adherence to protocol. But most of them are nervous; it's their first salon too. Carima casts a critical eye on Liam to make sure he is serving gracefully. To her irritation, his eyes are still locked broodingly on Colton. He's actually threatened: that's a first. Of course, he's never had to share her attention before. And being an exceptionally pretty boy, Liam's used to being the pick of the litter at any party. This is the first time another slave has challenged his confidence.

Colton seems aware of his effect, serving her tea with a slight smirk. "Like your boots," he murmurs.

Speaking to her is a violation of salon protocol. But he's giving her an open invitation to test Liam. "Thank you. They do make my feet ache..."

He's on his knees in a flash. "Allow me."

And just as he slips off her right boot and begins to massage the not-really-aching sole of her foot, a horrible clatter and shriek sound to the right.

Liam has spilled wine down another domme's leg.

"I'm sorry, fuck, I am so sorry," he mutters, swabbing ineffectively at her boot. The rest of the dommes and slaves stare in horrified amusement at the spectacle.

Carima wants to kill him. Instead she says calmly, "Into the dungeon, Liam."

His green eyes fill with fear but she doesn't relent. The dommes and slaves watch with curiosity as she slips on her boot and guides him into the adjoining dungeon by his neck.

She turns on the electric wall-mounted torches. She wasn't intending to use the dungeon tonight; this isn't a play party, just a salon. But Liam has embarrassed both of them and he must be punished.

She retrieves the chains she keeps chilled in the small dungeon freezer. Liam's color drains from his face but she marches him toward the menacing X of the St. Andrew's cross. "Lift your arms."

He lifts pleading eyes to her. Pinching his nipple hard, she repeats, "Lift your arms."

He obeys, never taking his eyes from the heavy, ice-cold lengths of chain. Carima refuses to let herself soften, shackling his arms to the upper points and following with his ankles on the bottom points, wrapping his body liberally with the chains. Liam shivers wildly, every inch of him naked, open and available.

His voice is miserable. "What—what are you going to do?"

"You don't get to ask me that," she retorts, giving his thigh a stinging smack of her crop.

He gives her a defiant look before dropping his gaze. She slides a black blindfold down over his eyes anyhow to intensify the sensation of helplessness. Then she gently traces the leather tip of her crop up his inner thigh.

"I thought you were ready for this."

"I am."

"You don't seem to be."

"I've just never been around other people when I'm..." His voice fades but she knows how to finish that sentence. *When I'm submissive, naked, helpless and hard.*

She doesn't reassure him. Instead she strokes his cock, palming the head until he moans, and says only: "Shiver for me."

Walking out of the dungeon, her mind flashes back to the fetish ball where they met. He had been the most beautiful boy in the room, but it was the passion and intelligence she noticed in his eyes as he watched her. She walked into a side room, knowing he'd follow. "On your knees," she said. He obeyed without a word. "Good. Now show me your cock." He unzipped his pants and let it spring free, hard and smooth and unmistakably hers. Then he shook back his blond hair and looked up with a desire that was both a challenge and an offer. She knew then that he was submissive, yes, but not servile. This boy was spirited. This was the slave she'd been waiting for.

Carima returns to the salon, leaving the dungeon doors open both to keep an eye on Liam and make a spectacle of him. But the salon has gone dull for her. The ladyfingers and fruit tarts seem silly and one of the slaves is serving the wine on ice. Anne's slave Marshall is so timid that his hands shake and the new slave Alejandro is so excited that he disappears into the bathroom for a suspiciously long time.

The dommes glance at each other. *It's the first one. They'll improve,* their eyes say. Carima agrees, but Liam's mishap has ruined the evening for her. She was so looking forward to showing him off tonight, from his gorgeous physique to his endearing manners. Instead he's fumbled like the fledgling she had hoped he no longer was.

Colton, ever brazen, brings her more wine. "I'll be everything your boy isn't," he mutters under his breath. Unbelievable. She's half-tempted to collar this kid and have him muck out her stable next weekend.

Night falls quickly. When the conversation winds down, Carima judges Liam has spent enough time in the dungeon. Beckoning the other dommes, she leads everyone into the adjoining room. The novice slaves gawk at the spanking bench, cage and swing, and the long row of paddles and canes. But the dommes gaze only at the naked spectacle of Liam blind-folded and chained on the cross. He looks so sexy in captivity, all hard muscles and stoic expression, his hair falling over his cheekbones. The chains have long since warmed and his cock has gone hard, as it always does in bondage. Lightly she reaches forward and trails her fingernails up his thick shaft. Immediately his stomach retracts and his thigh muscles go tight.

"Gorgeous," someone murmurs.

"Look at those abs," Anne says admiringly. "Some boys are just meant to be chained."

A loud scoff comes from across the room.

All of the dommes turn. Colton's smirk quickly vanishes and he looks submissively down at the floor. But it's too late. All of them have heard him express his contempt for Liam.

"Colton!" Stephanie scolds. "How rude. Mind your manners."

Mind your manners? How insipid, Carima thinks. "Colton, you've been defiant all evening, whispering to me when you should be serving and generally exhibiting an unacceptable insolence," she says. "You're setting a terrible example for the other boys."

"I'm sorry, Ma'am," Colton says in an abashed voice that doesn't fool her.

"Good. Then you will be disciplined now, or not invited back."

Colton's head jerks up with a startled expression.

Carima snaps her fingers. "Cross the room to the tool bench on your knees," she commands. "Hands locked on the back of your neck. Then bring me the paddle, still on your knees."

Stiffly he obeys. Watching him retrieve the paddle, she enjoys thinking of the rug burns he'll sport on those too-soft knees tomorrow. When he's returned to her, she pulls off Liam's blindfold and releases him from the cross, helping him down. He looks dazed and shaky.

"My arm is tired," she says casually, placing the paddle in his hand. "I think it will be much more humbling for Colton if *you* spank him, Liam."

Colton's dark eyes fill with outrage. Liam just looks stunned.

"Go on, do as I say," she orders. "Colton, bend over and grip the cross. And Liam, give it to him good."

Slowly, sullenly, Colton bends over to hold the cross and extend his bottom. His perfect ass is pale and unblemished by any earlier spankings, if indeed he's ever had one.

"Liam, give him twenty-five. Colton, you will count each one."

Liam shakes the lingering tension from his arms, then steps behind Colton's clenched white cheeks. The dungeon is silent. Every domme and every slave is riveted on the scene.

Liam lets loose with the first smack. Colton jumps a little. "One," he says through gritted teeth.

Liam delivers another blow on the other cheek. Colton almost straightens in protest before catching himself. "Two."

The rise and fall of the paddle goes on, punctuated by Colton's surly recitations. No one moves. Colton stares defiantly forward at first, but Liam knows how to draw it out, sensitizing his skin and changing the rhythm so he can never really adjust. By the tenth blow, the indignation in Colton's eyes is transforming into submission, until he's groaning with what sounds like as much lust as pain. Carima knows this will become one of her most arousing memories, watching her beautiful blond slaveboy spank an equally beautiful dark-haired slave.

Colton's long cock is stiff and dark with engorged blood. When at last he gasps, "Twenty-five," his arrogance is gone.

"Well. So you do respond to discipline." Carima takes the paddle from Liam. Colton's face is burning red with mortification but he can't hide his massive erection. "You might make a good slave yet."

"Thank you, Ma'am," he mutters and slinks away.

A heavy silence falls upon the room. At that moment, all of them seem to sense their first femdom salon is over. The slaves hastily clean up as the women finish their wine.

"The next one will be at my house," Anne says as they walk outside. "Maybe by the pool if it's warm enough."

"Sounds great," Carima agrees. She's pleased to have hosted the first. All told, it didn't go too badly; certainly everyone got a mouthwatering show.

The house is oddly quiet when she comes in. She snaps off the foyer lights and enters the living room to find Liam kneeling on the carpet, naked and hard, with his wrists cuffed before him and his mouth taped shut with a note that reads, USE ME.

He looks up at her with burning eyes.

"Oh, my aching god," she says. "You really do know just how to please me."

She walks around him in a circle, trailing her fingertips over his lateral muscles and caressing his silky hair.

"You don't ever need to be jealous of another sub," she says. "You're mine. You, and only you, belong to me."

She takes the tape off his mouth and rakes her nails over his lips, just enough to make his blood rise, before kissing him so passionately it's as if she wants to drown in him.

The windows are still open to the spring night. She lays him down on the carpet, deliberately positioning him so the damp breeze washes over one side of his naked skin while the heat of the flames beats on the other. He doesn't take his eyes from her as she slips out of her dress, bra and panties.

Liam tilts his head back in a clear invitation for her to sit on his face. Instead she grips his cock, twisting her hand around the swollen head until he moans. She knows exactly how to play him, how to make him shudder and scream and come like he's on fire. Tonight, though, she is thirsty for the taste of him and swallows his cock deep into her mouth. A desperate little whimper comes out of him as she tongues and sucks him, his hips dancing on the floor. The tangy-sweet taste of him tempts her to keep sucking, but the liquid fire building in her pussy urges her onward. She licks the slit of his cock and withdraws, laughing as he twists impatiently against his cuffs in frustration.

Now she does what she's wanted to ever since she watched him spank Colton. Taking his hard dick in hand, she straddles him and leans over to dangle her breasts in his face. Liam eagerly sucks her nipples into his mouth, but she allows herself the sensation of his tongue, so warm against the cool night air, for only a few moments before pulling away. He groans again and she slowly rubs her pussy against him. Biting her lip, she strokes the head of his cock up and down her wetness, tracing his crown over her soft folds until he groans.

"Please," Liam begs. She dips two fingers into her pussy then feeds them into his eager mouth as a reminder that he needs permission before speaking.

She moves back onto his shaft until she engulfs him completely. There it is, that blissful feeling of utter control:

her beautiful boy bound and helpless with his cock captured inside her.

A strangled noise of desire escapes him. Carima twists and moves on him, gripping him tightly with her muscles. Liam thrusts up at her from the carpet, trying to drive inside her. But she rides him at her will, fucking him faster and deeper until a fiery prickle of heat fills her nipples. They're thrusting in tandem now, in an urgent, primal rhythm she never wants to end. An intoxicating bliss fills her limbs like liquid fire. She moves his cuffed wrists between her legs and grinds her clit against his fingers, and as Liam groans and writhes beneath her, she comes in wet, euphoric shudders on his cock. A raw, searing cry escapes him and he erupts inside her, hips pumping out every throe of his orgasm.

Slowly Carima climbs off his hips. Her body feels as weightless and brilliant as fire itself. Only as she uncuffs him does she become aware of her own trembling.

She looks at him in the firelight, her young slave gleaming with sweat. "Are you mine?" she asks, tracing his bottom lip. "Tell me you belong to me."

"I'm yours." His green eyes gaze at her as if bewitched. "I'm yours completely."

She traces her nails down his thighs, then up to his throat, savoring the jump of his pulse. Another breeze comes through the window screen to race across her flushed skin, making her shiver.

"If you didn't already know, I belong to you too," she says at last.

Liam wraps his arms around her and holds her tightly as they bask in the heat of the flames.

ABOUT THE AUTHORS

VALERIE ALEXANDER lives in Arizona. Her work has been previously published in *Best of Best Women's Erotica, Best Bondage Erotica* and other anthologies.

LAURA ANTONIOU (LAntoniou.com) has been writing erotica for over twenty years. Best known for her *Marketplace* series, she has also edited and appeared in many anthologies. She has recently finished her first mystery, *The Killer Wore Leather*, and is working on book 6 of the *MP* series.

KATHLEEN BRADEAN's (KathleenBradean.Blogspot.com) stories can be found in *Carnal Machines, Spank!, The Harder She Comes, Best of Best Women's Erotica 1* and *2, Haunted Hearths and Sapphic Shades, The Sweetest Kiss* and many other anthologies. She blogs for Oh Get A Grip, and reviews erotica at EroticaRevealed.com.

JACQUELINE BROCKER (jacquelinebrocker.esquinx.net) is an Australian writer living in the UK. She is published by Filament Magazine, Every Night Erotica, Freaky Fountain Press (*Erotica Apocrypha*), and by Ravenous Romance (*My First Spanking*). Her other writing includes historically tinged fantasy and she also dabbles in crime fiction.

RACHEL KRAMER BUSSEL (rachelkramerbussel.com) is an author, editor and blogger. She has edited over forty anthologies, including *She's on Top; Yes, Ma'am; Please, Ma'am; Orgasmic; Fast Girls; Anything for You: Erotica for Kinky Couples; Spanked; Bottoms Up; Cheeky Spanking Stories* and the *Best Bondage Erotica* and *Best Sex Writing* series.

COLIN (gigglegasm.com) has written many ebooks for MTJ Publishing and has scripted the long-running MTJ fetish comics *Maggs, Lexi* and *Tammi the Tickle Witch*. Other Colin ebooks include *Laugh for Me, Tickle Toy, Soles in Torment,* and *Girlville.*

Called a "legendary erotica heavy-hitter" (by the über-legendary Violet Blue), **ANDREA DALE** (cyvarwydd.com) fears people dressed in giant animal costumes far more than public speaking. Her work has appeared in about one hundred anthologies from Harlequin Spice, Avon Red and Cleis Press, and is available online at Soul's Road Press.

ANNE GRIP lives in Brooklyn, NY and has been published in *Up All Night: Adventures in Lesbian Sex* and *Best Lesbian Erotica 2012.*

MIDORI is a San Francisco based educator and author. She travels far and wide, speaking on twenty-first-century sexuality to a wide range of audience—everything from colleges, the general public and the media to subculture groups. In 2001 she wrote the first English language book on Shibari, *The Seductive Art of Japanese Bondage*. Other books to date include *Wild Side Sex: The Book of Kink* and *Master Han's Daughter*. In 2002 she founded Rope Bondage Dojo©, leading many Dojos each year with the Dojo Cadre. Later she created ForteFemme, a unique women's dominance weekend training and empowerment intensive. Follow her on Twitter and Facebook at PlanetMidori.

EVAN MORA's stories of love, lust and other demons have appeared in anthologies like: *Please, Sir: Erotic Stories of Female Submission; Spank!; Best Bondage Erotica 2011; Bound by Lust: Romantic Stories of Submission and Sensuality* and *Cheeky Spanking Stories*. She lives in Toronto.

AIMEE NICHOLS is an erotic fiction author, burlesque performer and smut-brained sensualist living in Melbourne, Australia. You can visit her website at aimee-nichols.com or follow her on Twitter at @wordsandsequins.

Eroticist **GISELLE RENARDE** (wix.com/gisellerenarde/erotica) is a queer Canadian, avid volunteer, contributor to more than fifty short-story anthologies and author of dozens of electronic and print books, including *Anonymous, Ondine* and *My Mistress' Thighs*.

TERESA NOELLE ROBERTS writes romantic erotica and erotic romance for lusty romantics of all persuasions. Her work has appeared in *Best of Best Women's Erotica 2; Best Bondage*

Erotica 2012; Orgasmic; Spanked; Playing with Fire and other anthologies with similarly provocative titles. She writes erotic romance for Samhain and Phaze.

DOMINIC SANTI (dominicsanti@yahoo.com) is a former technical editor turned rogue whose stories have appeared in many dozens of publications, including *Surrender; Yes, Ma'am; Caught Looking; Hot Under the Collar; Indecent Proposals; Voyeur Eyes Only: Vegas Windows;* and *Red Hot Erotica.* Santi is currently working on a highly irreverent historical novel.

After thirteen years, **LISABET SARAI** has lost track of all her publications and their genres, but she's particularly partial to stories of power exchange. In addition to writing, she edits the single-author charity series *Coming Together Presents* and reviews erotica for Erotica Readers and Writers Association and Erotica Revealed.

LEELA SCOTT resides in Sacramento, California where she spends her free time bringing her erotic fantasies to life on the page. Her first published story appeared in *Spankalicious: Erotic Adventures in Spanking.*

T. R. VERTEN is the author of the erotic novella *Confessions of a Rentboy,* published by Republica Press. The best place to find her is on Twitter @trepverten where she talks about hot boys, her cats, and what's for dinner.

LAWRENCE WESTERMAN is a daydreamer and devoted submissive. He serves his wife of twenty-five years who he affectionately calls "Her Majesty." They live together in the Northeastern United States with their son and three cats. His blog (hermajestysplaything.blogspot.com) is devoted to the exploration of female domination and male submission.

VERONICA WILDE is an erotic romance author published with Cleis Press, Liquid Silver Books and Samhain Publishing. Please visit her at veronicawilde.com.

DAVID WRAITH is a Saint Louis native, writer, filmmaker and activist. He's a polyamorous sadomasochist and exhibitionist. He is one of the cofounders of Sex Positive St. Louis, and he occasionally rants about movies, sex and politics at davidwraith.com.

ANDREA ZANIN, aka Sex Geek, writes about alternative sexuality for numerous newspapers and magazines, blogs at sexgeek.wordpress.com and pens erotic fiction when she isn't working on her PhD. She lives in Toronto and enjoys cultivating M/s relationships with exceptionally high-quality individuals.

ABOUT
THE EDITOR

D. L. KING spends an inordinate amount of time reading and writing smut in her New York City apartment and postage stamp–sized garden. *Under Her Thumb: Erotic Stories of Female Domination* is her sixth anthology with Cleis Press. She is also the editor of *Seductress: Tales of Immortal Desire; The Harder She Comes: Butch/Femme Erotica*; The Independent Publisher Awards Gold Medalist, *Carnal Machines: Steampunk Erotica; The Sweetest Kiss: Ravishing Vampire Erotica* and the Lambda Literary Award Finalist, *Where the Girls Are: Urban Lesbian Erotica*. She is also the editor of *Spank!, Voyeur Eyes Only: Vegas Windows* and *Spankalicious: Adventures in Spanking*. D. L. King is the publisher and editor of the erotica review site, Erotica Revealed, which has been called the *New York Times Book Review* of Erotica. The author of dozens of short stories, her work can be found in various editions of *Best Lesbian Erotica; Best Women's Erotica; The Mammoth Book of Best New Erotica*; as well as such titles as *Girl Fever; Say*

Please; One Night Only; Power Play; Luscious; Hurts So Good; Fast Girls; Gotta Have It; Please, Ma'am; Sweet Love and *Frenzy*, among others. She is the author of two novels of female domination and male submission, *The Melinoe Project* and *The Art of Melinoe*. Find out more at dlkingerotica.blogspot.com and dlkingerotica.com.